a/io

A NOTE TO REA

While the Ramsey and Morgan families ... , the troubles faced by people living in Cincinnati during 1819 are all too true. Now known as a Midwestern city, Cincinnati in the early nineteenth century was part of America's western frontier. During the time of this story, Cincinnati's lifeblood, the Ohio River, was so low that boats couldn't travel on it. Many people lost their jobs, and many families went hungry.

At that time, states printed their own money. The value of the money varied from day to day, and when there were financial problems, the money often became worthless. This confusing situation caused many problems that took more than a hundred years to straighten out.

Because there weren't radios or televisions, musical instruments were very important forms of entertainment for families in the 1800s. Having a piano or parlor organ in the home became common, and by the end of the century, most girls were expected to know how to play the piano at least a little.

SISTERS IN TIME

Grace

and the Bully

DROUGHT ON THE FRONTIER

NORMA JEAN LUTZ

BARBOUR
PUBLISHING

Grace
and the Bully

To Gene and Barbara Yeager
The two of you are the epitome of the fruit of the Spirit gentleness.
I cherish your friendship.

© 2006 by Barbour Publishing, Inc.

ISBN 1-59789-102-9

Cover design by Lookout Design Group, Inc.

Published by Barbour Publishing, Inc., P.O. Box 719, Uhrichsville, Ohio 44683 www.barbourbooks.com

Our mission is to publish and distribute inspirational products offering exceptional value and biblical encouragement to the masses.

 Member of the
Evangelical Christian
Publishers Association

Printed in the United States of America.

5 4 3 2 1

CONTENTS

CHAPTER 1

Trouble at School

Excitement tumbled and bubbled deep inside ten-year-old Grace Morgan's stomach, making it difficult for her to pay attention. Her chin rested on her hand as she stared out the schoolhouse window.

The crowded classroom on the first floor of the brick building was not only noisy, but stuffy, too. The classroom upstairs, where the older students attended, was just as crowded. Thankfully, Grace's seat was by an open window, where she could feel the soft spring breeze blowing in. She didn't mind that she had to share a seat with Amy Coppock. Amy had been her friend for almost two years.

April meant that her fifth-grade school term was nearly over. That in itself was enough to make Grace want to turn handsprings. But today was much more exciting than the close of school. Tonight she and Mama would pen the order for her brand-new piano!

She'd dreamed of having a piano for months. Finally, Papa said that with the contracts for two new steamboats, there would be enough money for a piano. Grace sighed as she thought of the pictures in the catalog she and Mama pored over night after night. But now the decision was made. Papa said the steamboat *Velocipede* would be leaving in the morning, and the order would go onboard with the outgoing mail!

Shifting in the small, hard seat, Grace brought her attention to the front of the room, where Mr. Inman tried his utmost to work on recitation with a group of first- and second-grade students. Mr. Inman's stand-up white collar, which that morning had looked starched and spiffy, now looked rather wilted. His black bow tie drooped, as well.

Grace had decided months ago that Silas Inman was too kind and gentle to be a teacher, especially in this crowded room. The older boys talked out of turn and kept a ruckus rumbling most of the time. Last year's teacher, grouchy old Mr. Travers, seemed harsh and mean, but at least the boys had behaved.

Out of the corner of her eye, Grace saw Raggy Langler shoot a spitwad right at the back of her cousin Drew's head. Drew Ramsey sat two rows over with the sixth graders. Grace watched as he reached up to remove the wet mass from his hair and turned around to scowl at Raggy. Even from two rows over, she could sense Drew's disgust. Drew had told her there were never boys like Raggy in his school in Boston.

Poor Drew. Ever since he'd arrived from Boston two months ago, several of the boys had made fun of his dapper clothes and Boston accent, but Raggy was the worst. As Mr. Inman turned his back, Grace stuck her tongue out at Raggy, making Amy giggle. Raggy shook his fist at her and mouthed the threat, "I'll get you."

Grace just turned up her nose and ignored him. Amy nudged Grace, then pinched her own nose, indicating that Raggy smelled bad. Grace nodded in agreement. Raggy's dark hair was matted, his clothes were worn and frayed, and his neck was the color of dirty dishwater. His nose seemed too long for his angular face. The boy was continually scratching, and Grace was certain he must have lice.

On their shared slate, Amy and Grace were supposed to be

working their multiplication tables, but instead, Grace had drawn a stick-figure girl sitting at a piano. Amy knew all about the new piano that would soon be coming to the Morgan household, and she was happy for Grace.

"I wouldn't even want a piano," Amy had said that day at recess time. "Then Mama would make me practice every day. I'd hate that." She screwed up her pretty face at the very thought.

But Grace didn't see it that way. It was as though her fingers hungered to move over the smooth ivory keys and coax out melodies to accompany her singing.

Last year, the church her family attended had purchased a piano. But only Widow Robbins was allowed to go near the fine instrument. No one was even supposed to touch the dark mahogany lid to take a peek at the shiny row of black-and-white keys. Grace told Mama that was unfair. Mama just said, "Rules are rules, Gracie. You know that."

Now that Grace had celebrated her tenth birthday, she hated being called *Gracie*, but still Mama, Papa, and even her older brother, Luke, insisted on calling her that.

Just then, Mr. Inman finished with the younger children and called the class to order. His efforts were rewarded only slightly as the older boys continued to whisper and laugh. Raggy had a handful of followers who mimicked his every action, especially Wesley Smith and Karl Thompson.

"As we approach the closing of the school term—" Mr. Inman began. He was interrupted with cheers from Raggy and those around him.

"Yea, hooray!" they cried in chorus. "No more school!"

Mr. Inman's soft brown eyes were troubled as he surveyed the culprits. Tugging at his dark chin whiskers, he began again. "The superintendent of schools has asked that all classrooms have a presentation prepared for the closing-day ceremony. Be thinking of how our classroom can contribute to the program, either individually or as a group."

Amy's hand shot up, and when the teacher called on her, she said, "Grace Morgan can sing, Mr. Inman. She has the most beautiful voice in the world. Nicer than a nightingale."

Grace felt herself blushing. She had no idea Amy was going to blurt out such a thing. Often she sang for family gatherings. A few times she'd even sung at church. But singing in front of the entire community would be quite different.

"Thank you, Amy." To Grace, he said, "Would you please have a song prepared for the program, Grace?"

"Yes, sir," she answered, feeling giddiness building inside her. Now she had one more exciting thing to look forward to.

From the back of the room, Raggy said in a loud whisper, "Dapper-Dandy Drew could show us how to talk Yankee talk."

Drew's hair—the color of corn silk—didn't quite cover his ears, and Grace saw them turn red right up to the tips. How she wished she could do something to cheer up Drew. She tried to imagine what it would be like if she were to lose both her parents to such a wretched disease as yellow fever. That's what had happened to Drew just last winter.

Grace turned to give Raggy her worst scowl. He was such a beast.

Mr. Inman gave Raggy, whose name in class was *Russell*, a warning to keep silent, but the warnings carried little weight. Raggy mostly did whatever he wanted. And that seldom meant schoolwork.

In the past, Raggy had showed up for school only about half the time, but recently his attendance had become almost perfect. Grace believed that Raggy came to school only to take part in tormenting poor, defenseless Drew.

At last, Mr. Inman completed all the instructions regarding the school-closing ceremonies, which, he said, would include a parade down Main Street. Amy and Grace nudged one another at the prospect of a parade. What fun that would be!

Class was then dismissed, and Grace went to the cloakroom to fetch her tin pail from the shelf. Drew was right there beside her. Out in the schoolyard, Amy called out a good-bye as she and her older brother, Jason, headed west down Fourth Street toward their home. Grace often wished Amy lived nearer to Deer Creek so they could walk home together.

Before going out of the fenced schoolyard, Grace said to Drew, "Wait a minute." Sitting down in the dirt, she proceeded to unbutton her hightop shoes and pull off her long, itchy woolen stockings. The shoes, which had been purchased at the shoemaker's last autumn, were now much too tight.

"Grace, what are you doing?" Drew protested. "You can't walk barefoot in these filthy streets."

"Of course I can. Just watch me." She jumped up and wiggled her toes in the dirt, making little dust puffs. "*Ahh.* Now my feet are finally free."

Drew shook his head in disbelief. "No girl in Boston would walk home from school barefoot in the dirt." He paused a moment as he studied Fourth Street. It was nearly three inches deep in dirt. "But then, in Boston there are no dirt streets."

"Oh, come on, Drew," she said, hurrying on ahead of him and turning off Fourth Street to Walnut. "Forget about Boston for a while.

Let's go down near the landing and look at the *Velocipede* before going home." Grace wanted so much to help Drew forget about past things and for him to be as happy about Cincinnati as she was.

"I thought you weren't supposed to go near the landing by yourself," Drew countered, hurrying to catch up with her.

Grace gave a little giggle. "I'm not by myself, silly. You're with me. And besides, we won't go all the way to the landing. We'll just look down from Second Street."

She knew Drew wanted to hurry home. Among other things, Drew was frightened of the many pigs that ran wild on the streets. The helpful pigs ate the garbage that was thrown into the streets every day by the town's residents.

"I know you're wary of the pigs, Drew," she told him as patiently as she could. "But we'll find two big old sticks, and if any pigs come along, we'll just whack them on the snout."

Grace had never had a pesky pig attack her, but she knew other children had been attacked and seriously hurt. The gruesome stories had scared Drew.

Grace pointed to a yard where several large shade trees grew. "There should be a couple of sticks under those trees." But before they could head that direction, out from between two buildings came Raggy along with Wesley and Karl. They whooped and hollered.

"Dapper Drew! Dresses up in pretty clothes! Looks like a dandy!" Raggy called out in a singsong voice.

Quickly the other two took up the chant: "Dapper Drew! Looks like a dandy!"

Grace caught the look of fear in Drew's eyes. These boys were more frightening to him than a whole herd of pigs.

CHAPTER 2

The Fight

Grace stopped stock-still and turned about to glare at the trio. "You boys hush your mouths!" she demanded. "Leave us alone!"

Drew seemed confused, but Grace knew if he shot off running, they'd be after him for sure. "Pay 'em no mind at all, Drew Ramsey," she said in a loud voice. "At least your name is better than *Raggy*." She spit out the word with all the disdain she could muster.

But Raggy's attention was not on Grace. Coming closer, the tall boy reached down to grab a handful of the dirt from Walnut Street and flung it at Drew. "Now the dandy's a *dirty* little dandy," he said and roared with laughter.

"Stop that!" Drew protested. In vain he tried to brush off his nice navy coat and matching trousers. As Drew looked down at the mess, Raggy gave him a sudden shove, dumping him into the dirt.

Grace could stand it no more. She began twirling around, swinging her tin pail as she went. Coming up right behind Raggy, she whammed him in the back of the legs with the pail. Raggy yowled with pain. The blow knocked him off balance, causing him to stumble. As he did, he grabbed one of Grace's shoes that she'd dropped.

"Got your shoe!" he hollered as he ran off, but Grace was in hot pursuit.

"Stop that thief! He's a thief! Stop him!"

Not looking where he was going, Raggy ran smack into a well-dressed gentleman with a top hat and pearl-handled cane. "Here, here, you ragamuffin!" protested the man. "Watch where you're going!"

"Stop him!" Grace kept yelling. But Raggy threw the shoe as hard as he could and raced on down the street. His friends had long since disappeared.

With the help of the kind stranger, Grace retrieved her shoe from within the high wrought-iron fence of a fine home, then retraced her steps to where Drew stood waiting.

"You know, Drew," she said as she tried to catch her breath, "if we stick together, we can whip that terrible Raggy Langler."

But even as she said it, she could tell Drew had no desire to whip anyone—even someone who'd pushed him into the dirt. It was as though there were no life in her cousin at all.

"Why do they allow ruffians like him to attend our school?" Drew wanted to know. "He should stay in Sausage Row where he belongs."

Drew was referring to the run-down district near the landing where the poorer people of the city lived.

"Papa says the city voted to pay the way for a few indigent children to attend as well as those of us who *can* pay the subscription to go to school." Grace felt proud to know these facts, but it was only because she sometimes sat on the stair landing and listened to the grown-ups talk. She was always sent to bed before serious talk began.

"But why someone like Raggy?" Drew asked. "He doesn't even want to learn."

"It's because of the washerwoman he lives with. Emaline Stanley is her name. She took Raggy in when she found him roaming around Sausage Row all alone. I hear tell she's plumb set on him getting educated." Grace chuckled. "They say she barged right into a meeting of the board of trustees to have her say."

Drew shook his head. "Doesn't she realize the boy's not worth it?"

"I guess not. You know, Drew, the Reverend Danforth says we're supposed to love everybody, but I don't see how anyone could love that dirty, mean-mouthed Raggy."

As they talked, they approached the brink of the hill. Walnut Street, like most of the north–south streets in town, led down toward the public landing at the bank of the grand Ohio River.

Grace loved the sight of the landing as it spread out before them. The wide cobblestone landing was flanked on the north by a row of stately buildings, housing factories, mills, and warehouses that thrived on the river business. At one end of the landing was the brick factory, at the other end was the glassworks.

Situated on the far side of the glassworks was the boatbuilding business in which Papa and Luke were involved. Papa had told her many times, "Grace, someday you'll see dozens, and perhaps even scores, of steamboats plying these waters. And mark my words, the queen city of Cincinnati will be smack dab in the middle of it all!"

The awe and thrill in Papa's voice never failed to stir something inside of Grace. How she wished Drew could be as impressed by this growing frontier city as she was.

"There it is!" she cried out as they approached Front Street. "There's the *Velocipede*!" The queenly steamboat sat high and proud near the landing, among lesser keelboats, barges, and a few meager flatboats, which carried individual families and all their earthly belongings.

"You see steamboats most every day," Drew commented dryly. "Nothing to get worked up about."

"But this steamboat will carry the order for my new piano!" she said, bouncing up and down on her bare toes.

Drew stopped beside her to study the river. "Why is the stern-wheeler out so far?" he asked.

Now Grace stopped to look, as well. "The water's low. Papa says it's because there was so little snow last winter and so little rain this spring."

"What happens if the water goes lower?"

Papa and Luke had told Grace about a summer many years ago when the river was dry for a number of months. But that was before they depended on steamboats to bring so many supplies from New York and New Orleans.

"It won't go any lower," she assured him—and assured herself, as well. "The spring rains will come soon. Just wait and see. Then, instead of complaining about the dust in the streets, you'll complain about all the mud." Grace didn't even want to think about the prospect of a business slowdown on Cincinnati's public landing, especially if it meant a slowdown on the arrival of her piano.

The walk to Front Street had taken them a few blocks out of the way in their journey home. Before turning to walk back up the hill to Third, Grace sat down to put on her shoes and stockings so Mama would never know she'd been running barefoot all over the city.

Looking up at Drew, she asked, "Are you going to do something special for the school program, Drew?" She hopped up as they resumed their walk toward home.

Drew gave a shrug.

"You told me you learned Greek and Latin in Boston. Why don't you recite a piece in Greek?" She laughed as she thought of it. "That'd show that old Raggy a thing or two." But she could see her great idea sparked little response in Drew. If she could speak another language, she'd teach it to Amy. Then they could talk about Raggy, and he'd never know what they were saying.

They were almost to the two-story brick home where Grace lived on Symmes Street. She stopped a moment at their front gate, where her mama had planted masses of rambling roses and honeysuckle bushes.

"In the morning, Papa and I will take the order for my piano down to the steamboat," Grace said. "If you want to go with us, come by earlier than usual."

Drew nodded in agreement. "Bye," he said giving her a listless wave.

Grace watched as he walked slowly toward the plank-covered log cabin situated in a clearing near Deer Creek. There, Drew lived with his older brother, Carter; Carter's wife, Deanna; and their two little ones, Adah and Matthew. Even though Carter had built a loft for Drew, Grace knew that, with two toddlers underfoot, it was a crowded place.

Opening the gate, she gave a sigh. It just didn't seem right that she should be so happy and Drew so sad. Although Drew's bedroom in the loft was nice, it was no doubt shabby in comparison to the fine room and fancy furnishings he'd enjoyed in Boston.

As she approached the front door, she could smell the wonderful aroma of her mama's beef stew. She burst into the roomy kitchen, where Mama was bent over the butcher-block table, stirring batter in a crockery bowl.

"Mama," she called out, "I'm home!"

Mama looked up and brushed a strand of chestnut-colored hair from her forehead with the back of her hand. "Gracie, what happened to you? Your bonnet's down and your hair's a fright!"

From the pantry, Grace heard snickers from Regina Watson, their hired girl. Grace ignored the snickers since it seemed Regina was always laughing at her. Quite honestly, Grace had forgotten that her bonnet had fallen back during her wild encounter with Raggy.

"Too much running at recess, I guess," she said quickly. She decided not to tell Mama about the chase, especially not while Regina was listening.

Just then, Regina emerged from the pantry carrying two pies. She was a thin girl with stringy hair and a mousy face. "Gracie is forever running," she said. "A few chores would settle her down, I'd say."

Regina accused Grace of being petted because she was the youngest. If Grace weren't so polite, she'd tell Regina that Luke had called the hired servant "an addlepated girl with half the sense God gave a goose." Instead, she simply ignored Regina. Hugging her mother, she breathed deeply the aromas of yeasty dumpling batter.

"Go wash your hands and brush your hair, then come and tell me about your day," said Mama.

Grace pinched off a tiny bit of dough and popped it into her mouth. Her news couldn't wait until after a washing. "Mama," she said, "you'll never guess what—I'm going to sing at the school-commencement exercises!"

Mama stopped stirring batter now and raised her eyebrows. "Why, fancy that, our little Gracie singing in front of all those people!"

Regina came to take the bowl from Mama's hands and began dropping spoonfuls of the batter into the boiling stew.

"Mama, please," Grace protested. "I'm not 'Little Gracie' anymore. I'm ten years old." She leaned against the heavy butcher-block table and went back to her story. "It was because of Amy that I was asked. She told Mr. Inman that I have a beautiful voice."

"And you certainly do." Mama waved her flour-covered hand. "Now go do as I said, please."

Backing away toward the kitchen door, Grace added, "Will you and Papa help me choose the perfect song to sing?"

Mama nodded as she turned to dip her floured hands in a basin of water and wipe them on a linen towel. "We'll talk at supper," she said. "Go on now."

"And after supper we'll write out the piano order?"

Mama looked up and smiled her warm, kind smile. "That's exactly what we're going to do."

Grace almost slipped and said she'd looked at the *Velocipede*, but she caught herself in the nick of time. She wasn't supposed to come home by way of Front Street.

Strolling out of the kitchen, Grace gazed down the hallway at the brand-new parlor Papa had built just last year. When it was finished, Mama had purchased flowered wallpaper at the mercantile store and had it hung, along with heavy dark green drapes. Between the what-not shelves and the fireplace was the very spot where Grace's piano would sit. By using her imagination just a bit, she could actually see it sitting there and see herself running her fingers over the keys. She could even see pages and pages of music on the stand.

Halfway up the stairs, she hung out over the balustrade to gaze again at the empty space on the carpet where the piano would be placed. In just a few months it would be there. She could hardly wait!

CHAPTER 3

The Piano Order

The oil lamp made a warm golden glow in the center of the dining table as Mama laid out the quill, ink, sand, and paper. There, too, was the flickering candle to use for sealing wax.

"We'll work at the table," Mama said, "so we can sit together. There's room for only one person at the secretary."

All the fixings from dinner had been cleared away. Regina had gone home, taking a few of the leftovers with her in her wicker basket. Grace was quite thankful that Regina did not live with them.

Mama spread out the catalog to the page they'd marked. "Now, you're sure this is the one?" she asked.

Grace nodded, so excited she could barely speak. "I'm sure."

The handsome-looking piano was mahogany and looked every bit as nice as the one at church. *Just let cranky Widow Robbins have her old piano,* Grace thought. But she would never say such a thing out loud.

Mama picked up the quill to dip in the ink.

"May I, Mama? May I write the order?"

Mama looked surprised. "Why, I suppose you can." She handed the quill to Grace. "I'll read out the words and numbers."

Writing the order made Grace feel just like a grown woman.

Why couldn't Mama and Papa remember how grown-up she was becoming?

When they were finished, Mama said, "Thad, would you come here a minute? We're ready for the banknote."

Grace's broad-shouldered papa seemed to fill the room when he entered. He pulled out the other cane-bottomed chair and sat down.

"Let's see here now," he said, picking up the order. "My, my. Would you look at Gracie's beautiful penmanship?"

Grace wanted to protest again about being called *Gracie*, but it seemed easier to say so to Mama than Papa. Papa always looked at her with a merry twinkle in his eye. "Thank you, Papa," she said instead.

"By the time the leaves turn and the pawpaws are ripe, we'll have a house filled with music."

"We already have a house filled with music, Papa," Grace countered. "Your fiddle does that."

Papa reached out to gently pat her arm. "Now, I'm trusting that you'll be making music much more grand than my screechy old fiddle."

Grace laughed at his joke, but she thought his fiddle music was wonderful.

She watched as Papa's strong hand took the quill to write out the banknote for a partial payment. Because of Papa's successful boatbuilding business, he had a great deal of money now in the Branch Bank at Fourth and Vine.

"Lavina," she'd heard him say to Mama just last week, "when the two steamboats that Luke and I are building now are finished, we'll be just about as wealthy as Chesman Billings."

The very thought made Grace gasp. Mrs. Chesman Billings had come to Mama's sewing circle one time. Grace had never seen such an elegant and stylish dress as this lady of wealth had worn. Mr. Billings's landholdings in the city of Cincinnati were extensive. Amy's father also owned several prime lots along Fourth Street. Perhaps one day Grace and Papa and Mama would live in a fine house farther up on the hill.

"Here you go, Gracie," Papa said, handing her the note. Carefully she folded it inside the order and Mama helped her secure it with sealing wax. On the outside of the paper, she penned the address of the piano factory in New York, carefully wiping the quill when she was finished.

"This occasion calls for a celebration," Papa said. "How about a song before going to bed?"

Moving to the parlor, Papa took his fiddle down from the special shelf he'd made. After tuning the strings, he struck up a merry tune that he'd learned from a keelboatman. Grace sang all the verses, with Mama and Papa joining in harmony on the chorus:

The boatman is a lucky man,
No one can do as the boatman can,
The boatmen dance and the boatmen sing,
The boatman is up to everything.
Hi-O, away we go,
Floating down the river on the O—hi—o.

Grace rolled up the carpet and danced a jig as she'd seen the swarthy boatmen do. From her favorite spot on the bluff high above where Deer Creek emptied into the Ohio, she often watched the keelboats and the larger heavy barges moving up and down the river. Traveling upstream meant teams of muscular rowers must work the long oars. On top of the low, boxy cabin sat the fiddler, sometimes wearing a slouch hat upon his head and a bright bandanna at his neck. The boatmen rowed to the rhythm of the fiddler's music. But when the way was easy traveling downstream, the boatmen passed the time dancing jigs. The happy tunes and fancy steps stayed inside Grace's head.

Mama laughed when they finished the last verse and the final rousing chorus. "When your piano is here, Grace, perhaps our music will consist of something other than boatmen ditties."

Grace nodded. "I'll learn church hymns, Mama," she agreed. "But I'll always love the happy boatmen songs."

Later, as Papa opened the big family Bible and read the scriptures, Grace's thoughts turned to Drew's problem that day with Raggy Langler. When they prayed, she asked Papa to say a special prayer for Drew to be happy.

Drew sat at the small table in the center of the cabin. Bent over his Latin textbook, he read the words by the flicker of the lamp. Matthew and Adah were at last quietly sleeping on the trundle bed. When the little ones were awake, Drew found concentration impossible.

He tried to read several pages of Latin every evening. Sometimes, if he had the time and the extra paper, he meticulously worked on translations. One time Deanna asked him why he worked so hard on his Latin studies, but Drew found he just couldn't explain. "I like Latin," was all he said.

It was as though he owed it to his father and mother. His parents had made sure he had the finest education that Boston could offer; now it was upon him to maintain what he'd received. And it certainly wasn't going to happen at the crowded school he currently attended.

Once, he'd called it a "charity school" in front of Grace, and she'd become upset. "It is not a charity school," she protested. "It's a public school. Papa pays a subscription just like everyone else."

Drew hadn't meant to hurt his cousin's feelings, because he liked Grace. But he knew the amount of subscription was a paltry sum. After all, the concept of the school was to cater to all—even creatures such as Raggy Langler.

Drew's older brother, Carter, sat across from him, polishing and cleaning his musket and filling the room with the aroma of flaxseed oil. The small cabin seemed to shrink when Carter was there. His very presence loomed over Drew like a shadow. Because Carter had been away from Boston for so many years, Drew barely knew him. They were worlds apart. It was strange, but Drew felt lonelier when his brother was home than he did when he was away.

"Drew," Deanna said softly, "it's time you were in bed."

"Yes, ma'am," Drew answered politely. Closing his book, he went to the basin near the cabin door, poured a little water from the pitcher, and washed his face and hands. There was lye soap nearby, but he hesitated to use it unless he was really dirty. He felt guilty using the family's supplies. His older brother had come to Cincinnati with nothing and had worked hard to eke out a living. Even now they had little to spare. Drew felt he was just another mouth to feed.

As Drew moved to the ladder that led to his loft, Deanna came to put her arm about his shoulder. "Sleep well, Drew."

"Thank you."

Her touch, which felt so like his mother's, made hot tears burn in his eyes. He turned away and blinked them back.

Carter said, "Good night, Drew." But he never looked up from his prized gun.

Back home in Boston, when his parents were still alive, they closed each evening with scripture reading and prayers—but Carter seemed to have forgotten all about God—except to accompany his family to church each Sunday. Pulling off his waist shirt and breeches and pulling on his nightshirt, Drew wondered himself if God were still around.

Lying on his small cot, he stared through the semidarkness at the slanted roof just a few feet above his head. Drew sighed. From beneath his pillow, he brought out the smooth piece of wood that he was carving with his sharp penknife. Father had told Drew many times that he had just the right touch to make a piece of wood come alive.

Now that the days were longer and light came in the small window, he often carved and whittled after going to bed. But tonight he was too tired. Holding up the wood in the shadows of the loft, he smiled. The shape was that of a sleek cod-fishing schooner such as those docked in Boston Harbor. Carving the ship helped him to remember Boston.

Just then, he remembered he was to leave for school earlier the next morning. Climbing out of the bed and moving to the ladder, he called down softly, "Deanna?"

"Yes, Drew?"

"Will you wake me earlier in the morning? I'm to go to the

27

landing with Grace and her father before school."

"I'll rouse you," Carter answered, "when I go out to cut the wood."

"Thank you," Drew said and returned to bed. Carter's words were like a slap. When Drew first arrived in Cincinnati, Carter had asked him to split kindling, but Drew had never swung an ax in his life. Although Drew was more than willing to learn, Carter had no patience to teach him.

"You might get your clothes dirty," Carter had said.

The comment cut deeply. Drew had no other clothes to wear. While he'd seen many well-dressed men, especially around the business district of Fourth Street, he was dressed differently than most of the other boys.

In the low bureau at the foot of his cot were the portraits of Mother and Father. Father had commissioned them to be painted only a few months before they died. Sometimes Drew allowed himself to take them out and look. But very rarely. . .and only when he was alone. He never wanted his brave older brother to see him cry.

He had very nearly cried that afternoon when Raggy attacked him. In the darkness, Drew smiled as he remembered the sight of Grace swinging her tin pail with all her might.

While Drew hated having a girl stand up for him, he appreciated Grace's friendship. He knew she was on his side. She didn't have to invite him to come to the steamboat with her in the morning. He would have to remember to thank her for her kindness.

Drew was happy that Grace invited him, but he knew being near a steamboat might remind him of the sad journey down the Ohio a few months ago. He'd have to be careful not to cry. Again.

CHAPTER 4

News from the Landing

A light patter of rain was falling when Grace heard Drew's knock at the kitchen door the next morning. He was early. She and Mama and Papa hadn't finished breakfast yet.

Grace left her place at the table to answer his knock. "Come in," she said. Drew's solemn face lit up as he smelled the aroma of Mama's flapjacks.

"Good morning, Drew!" Mama called out. Without asking, Mama fetched another plate from the cupboard. "You might as well have a few flapjacks and a slice of ham while you wait."

Drew sat down at the table without being asked twice. By the time Grace had gone upstairs to fetch her cloak with the hood, Drew had polished off the plate of food. Grace wondered if he'd had much breakfast at Carter's house.

She'd heard Luke and Papa talking about Carter. When Carter had first arrived in Cincinnati, he'd worked at the boatworks for a short time but then decided to go out on his own as a tanner. What he didn't take into account was that there were already more than a dozen tanyards and no need for a new one. He hadn't done as well as he'd hoped, so Papa had offered to let him come back to the boatworks. Carter had turned down the offer. Papa had told Luke, "Carter is too proud."

Maybe Carter doesn't have enough money to feed Drew properly. That thought worried Grace. Carter worked some days at the tanyard. Other days he chopped wood and went hunting in the nearby forests.

She learned these things while sitting on the stair landing, listening to the grown-ups talk.

"Thank you for the breakfast, Aunt Lavina!" Drew called to Mama, as he followed Papa and Grace out the door.

Grace figured there wasn't a more polite boy than Drew in the whole state of Ohio.

The landing was a busy place. Horses whinnied as they pulled wagons full of boxes, bags, and barrels close to the boat for unloading. Black stevedores shouted to one another and tossed about heavy bags of flour as though they were feather pillows. Several fine carriages, harnessed with smart-stepping horses, were hitched nearby as passengers said good-bye to friends and family in preparation to embark.

Papa was a friend of the captain of the *Velocipede*, so he strode up the broad gangplank as though he had a ticket to ride all the way to Pittsburg, Pennsylvania. Captain Micah Wharton was down on deck, greeting passengers and overseeing the loading so all was done in an orderly manner.

"Top o' the morning to you, Thad Morgan!" Captain Wharton called out when he saw Papa. Grace liked the captain's cheery voice, his ruddy red cheeks, and his broad, thick mustache. "And here's Gracie, too. To what do I owe this special visit?"

After introducing Drew to the tall captain, Papa explained, "Grace has a letter to go in the mailbag, Captain Wharton."

The captain raised his bushy eyebrows. "It must be terribly

important to be hand-delivered to the captain."

Grace was bursting to tell. She held up the folded and sealed letter. "It's my order for a new piano! It's coming from a factory in New York."

"Is that a fact?" the captain reached out his large, big-boned hand. "I'll see to it that it's delivered safely." He slipped the order into the pocket of his greatcoat with its shiny brass buttons. Looking wistfully out at the river, he added, "If we don't get a little rain, we may not see you again until this time next year."

Hearing those frightful words, Grace stopped still. But then came Papa's reassuring voice. "See those clouds?" Papa waved to indicate the overcast skies. "The Lord willing, the spring rains will come. And probably too much, as usual. That's the way it seems to happen around here."

Captain Wharton shook his head. "I want to think you're right, Mr. Morgan, but. . ." Just then, the captain's attention was diverted. "Hey there!" he yelled out to a carriage that had just pulled up and blocked the loading area. "Excuse me, folks. I must go see about this." And he was gone.

Grace turned around to see Drew standing by the deck railing, running his fingers gently over the carved and polished wood. There was that sad look on his face again. Adjusting her tin pail on her arm beneath her long cloak, she went over to stand beside him.

"Do you like steamboats?" she asked.

"I suppose so. That is, I like the way they're made. Especially the fancy woodwork."

Papa walked up behind them. "Time for you two to scoot off to school."

Grace looked up at Papa. "But I wanted to say good morning to

Luke since we're so close. May I, please, Papa?"

Grace's older brother, Luke, was one of her favorite people in the whole world. When Luke took pretty Camille for his bride, Grace wept. She was jealous of Camille for taking Luke away from her. But now the hurt was almost gone. Sometimes she was allowed to go to Luke and Camille's new home and stay overnight. That was fun.

Papa was looking at her with a twinkle in his eye. "Only if you promise to stay just a moment, then run on to school. You don't want to be responsible for making Drew late."

Following Papa's long strides down the wide cobblestone landing, Grace looked through the raindrops at the row of tall three- and four-story buildings that lined the landing. Each one was home to a thriving business. She wanted to comment on them to Drew, but she saw he wasn't noticing them at all. Drew was glancing wistfully back at the steamboat.

At the boatworks, the skeletal frames of the two new steamboats were taking shape. Nearby stood a large building where Luke oversaw the work on the steam engines. Luke was standing outside, talking to the men who were working on the boat frames.

When they called out to him, he turned. Running to lift her up and swing her around, he said, "Gracie! What are you doing at the landing? This is a school morning."

Once he'd set her down, Grace explained about the order for her brand-new piano.

"Ah, so you're finally getting your piano? Papa's little pet," he teased. "I suppose if you wanted the scepter from the king of Prussia, he'd get that for you, too."

"Oh, Luke, that's not true. When I learn to play, the piano will be for all the family. You can come and listen."

Luke screwed up his face and stuck his fingers in his ears. "And listen to you play sour notes? Not on your life."

She started to smack him but couldn't get her arm out of her cloak before he jumped, laughing, out of her reach.

Papa had been talking to his workers, but now he turned to tell Grace and Drew to get on their way. "You'll have to hurry now."

"Yes, Papa." Grace turned to see Drew picking up scrap pieces of wood and slipping them into his pocket. Drew was handy with his penknife. She'd seen the whistles and tops he'd carved for Matthew and Adah.

"Come on, Drew!" she hollered to him. "I'll race you up the hill!"

If Drew really tried, Grace was sure he could easily win the race. But he gave the race only a halfhearted try. By the time they reached the schoolhouse, huffing and puffing, the gray clouds had broken apart and the warm sun was out.

Later that morning at recess, Grace told Amy about the incident the day before with Raggy.

"How I wish you walked home the same direction as Jason and me," Amy said. "With Jason around, Raggy would never bother you or Drew."

Grace knew that was true. Even though Raggy Langler was big for his age, Jason was bigger. How nice it would be to have a guardian nearby like Jason Coppock.

Amy leaned toward Grace and confided, "Mama says that when Raggy was younger, he helped deliver wash for Emaline Stanley. Now all he does is run loose all over town and cause mischief."

Emaline was the washerwoman for Amy's family, so Amy would know. Grace shook her head at the thought of dirty, lazy Raggy.

"And helping Emaline with the deliveries is the least he could do for being allowed to live in the lean-to behind her shack."

Tired of talking about Raggy Langler, they turned their conversation to the school program and the pretty new dresses they would wear.

"If I had to stand before the entire city to sing, I'd be petrified," Amy said.

"I'm excited and a little nervous," Grace said, "but I'm not afraid." It was difficult to explain just how much she loved singing in front of people.

Suddenly, loud shouts sounded from a far corner of the playground. Looking that direction, Grace felt her heart sink. Raggy, Wesley, and Karl had Drew cornered near the fence and were taunting him. Other boys stood around laughing. Grace hated the onlookers for not helping Drew.

"Come on, Amy," she said. "Drew needs our help."

"You go," Amy said. "I have an idea."

Without a look back, Grace ran quickly toward Drew, yelling at the boys to get away and leave him alone.

Raggy stopped and glared at her. "Fellows, this little wildcat-gal's the one that smacked me on the legs."

"Yes, and I'd do it again as quick as you can draw a breath, Raggy Langler," Grace told him.

With attention shifted away from him, Drew tried to make a break, but Karl and Wesley blocked his escape. "Oh, no you don't, dapper-boy," Karl mocked.

Raggy gave a raspy laugh and spit a stream of " 'baccy juice," as he called it. "Our fancy boy here needs a little gal to come rescue him. *Tsk, tsk*," he said through his teeth. "Ain't that a sight?"

Just as Grace despaired that nothing but the recess bell could save Drew, a shout sounded behind her. "Get on out of here, you no-good scalawags!"

Jason Coppock was striding forcefully toward Raggy, and following him was Amy, sporting a wide grin!

CHAPTER 5

Yost's Mercantile

At the sight of the taller, stronger boy coming toward them, Wesley and Karl fled. Raggy stood his ground for a moment, calling after his pals not to run, but it was no use. They were gone.

"Go on," Jason said to Raggy. "Slither out of here like your two snaky friends. And in the future, pick on someone your own size."

"Just you wait." Raggy shook his fist at Drew, whose face was as white as a bedsheet. "I'll get you when you ain't got no little gal to hide behind." With that, he ran off to another part of the schoolyard.

"Well, what're you looking at?" Jason said sternly to the other boys standing about. Suddenly the crowd melted away.

Once Drew could find his voice, he thanked Jason.

"Think nothing of it," Jason said smiling.

"I don't know why those boys dislike me so," Drew said, his voice still shaky. "I've done nothing to harm them."

Jason laughed. "That has nothing to do with it, my friend. Ruffians like that are always looking for fresh prey. You just happen to be it."

Drew shook his head as though he couldn't believe it.

"You're from Boston, as I remember it." Jason had his arm about Drew's shoulder and was leading him to a shade tree where they sat down on the grass. "Surely you had Raggy's kind in Boston."

"Not where I lived," Drew said quietly.

"Well, let me tell you about boys like Raggy. All you have to do is stand your ground, and they'll hightail it. Every time."

While Drew politely thanked Jason for the advice, Grace could see he wasn't truly convinced. It was just like when she told him that a smart smack on a pig's snout would send it running. He simply didn't believe her.

The clanging of the bell broke into the conversation, and soon they were standing in their straight lines, ready to march to their classrooms. Grace gave Amy a wink and a grin as they saw Raggy trailing at the end of the line. With a friend like Jason Coppock, Grace reasoned, perhaps Drew would learn to laugh and have some fun.

Saturday was Grace's favorite day of the week. No school meant she could go to the market with Mama. The busy marketplace was filled with wagonloads of meat and produce from the outlying farms. Grace loved the sights and sounds and the hustle and bustle. Often she'd asked for permission to do the market shopping alone. "I can do it, Mama," she'd say. "I've watched you, and I know how to find the firmest heads of cabbage and the plumpest plucked hens."

But Mama always said no. "You're too little to shop alone. Some of the merchants in the market can't be trusted."

But earlier this week, Grace had tried a new approach. She had asked that Drew go along and that Mama allow the two of them to do the shopping. "Perhaps Drew can make purchases for Deanna," Grace had suggested. Once Grace saw she had Mama's full attention, she added, "Deanna would surely welcome such help."

When at last Mama gave in and reluctantly gave permission, Grace realized she'd not even asked Drew. When she did ask him, he seemed willing enough. At least Grace was right about Deanna.

"What a relief it will be not to have to make my way through the crowds with two little ones in tow," she said.

So it was settled. Before dawn on Saturday morning, Drew was at the Morgans' back door with Deanna's list in his hand and a basket on his arm. Mama instructed Grace several times about how to dicker for the best prices.

"When you've finished at the market," she added, "please stop at Yost's Mercantile for a paper of pins and a yard of sprigged muslin."

To the store, as well! Grace could hardly believe her good fortune. This made her feel more grown-up than ever.

The sky behind the hills to the west of the city showed barely a smudge of pink as Drew and Grace walked toward the lower market. A broad roof covered most of the area between Main and Sycamore and was supported by triple rows of brick pillars. But the sides were all open.

Since Drew had never before seen an open-air market, Grace showed him around and introduced him to the merchants she knew. Many of the farmers drove their wagons through the dark of night to vie for prime positions at the market. Feeling quite important, Grace taught Drew how to squeeze the cabbages to be sure they were not rotten in the center.

"Wait until summer, when the grapes come in," she told him as she chose a fat hen hanging from the racks. "There will be great baskets full of them, and you eat until you cannot eat any more." Talking about the juicy grapes made her mouth water.

"I'm not sure Deanna's budget could purchase that many grapes," Drew commented.

Grace wanted to say that Carter could earn fine wages at the boatworks, but she held her tongue. After all, Drew wasn't responsible for Carter's actions.

At Mr. Koenig's wagon, she found the firmest cabbages, and at Mr. Frey's wagon, she purchased the eggs. In her basket was a linen towel in which she was to wrap the eggs. Just as they were walking back through the rows of jammed-in wagons, Grace whispered, "Look there, Drew. It's Raggy Langler."

Raggy was slinking about the edges of the market area. As they watched, he slipped up to the back end of a wagon, reached in to grab a large white turnip, and then fled.

Grace gave a loud *whoop* and pushed through the crowd in that direction. "Stop that boy! He's a thief!" But no one was quick enough, and Raggy was long gone.

Leaving the market, they walked up Main toward Fourth Street and Yost's Mercantile. Muttering under his breath, Drew said, "It must be awful to have to steal for food."

Grace looked over at Drew in surprise. He sounded almost as though he felt sorry for Raggy. She knew she'd never steal, no matter how little she had. Wanting to change the subject, she said, "Mama gave me enough extra for each of us to have a stick of peppermint. You like peppermint, don't you?"

"Who wouldn't like peppermint?" he answered dully.

Grace was convinced nothing could ever excite Drew.

The heavy door of the mercantile was propped open, but the fresh spring air couldn't soften the strong mixtures of aromas inside the store. Here one could find everything from ax heads and kegs of nails to buggy whips and bolts of cloth. The store was fairly bristling with business.

Once inside, Grace was surprised to see Jason Coppock with a broom in his hands, sweeping the wooden floor. When he greeted them with a smile and a wave, Grace noticed that Drew brightened some.

"Amy never told me you worked for the Yosts," Grace said.

"I just started today." Jason waved his hand at all the merchandise and added, "Until I learn where everything is, I'm doing odd jobs. But soon I'll be a clerk." There was a note of pride in his voice. "Hey, Mr. Yost," he called over to a scar-faced man behind the counter. "We have a couple of customers here."

"Hi, Grace, Drew," Zachariah Yost greeted them cheerily. "What can I do for you today?" In spite of his terribly scarred face, Mr. Yost was a kind man and a good friend of Grace's brother, Luke.

Grace pulled out her list. "Mama needs a paper of pins and a yard of sprigged muslin."

"Pins and muslin, coming right up," he said. Pulling down the bolt of cloth and laying it on the counter, Mr. Yost asked, "How's your brother Luke doing these days? I don't see him much anymore."

"He and Papa are working hard to finish the two steamboats as soon as possible. Mama says they barely take time to breathe," Grace answered.

Mr. Yost chuckled at her comment. Carefully he measured and cut the muslin, folding the piece and returning the bolt to the shelf. "Now just tell me what those big old boats are gonna float on?" he asked. "From the looks of things, the river'll be down to a trickle in a few more weeks."

Grace didn't want to hear those words. True, there still hadn't been any hard spring rains, but they would come. She was sure of it. "Papa says the spring rains are just late," she told him.

"Late, huh? Well, I guess the snows were late, too. Don't forget, Gracie, there was very little snow all winter. Maybe the snows will come in June to raise the river level," he joked.

Grace quickly changed the subject. "Drew and I would each like a peppermint stick, as well, please."

"Two peppermint sticks." He added the items to the list, then took the wide-mouth jar from a shelf and brought it down to the counter where they could choose their own.

After Grace paid Mr. Yost, Drew suggested they put the cloth and pins in his basket since it wasn't as full as hers.

"Good idea," Grace agreed. "Now let's get on home and show Mama what a good job we've done."

As they moved toward the door, Jason called out, "Has Raggy Langler bothered you anymore?"

Grace answered by telling him they'd seen Raggy swiping vegetables at the market earlier.

Jason nodded. "I'd suspect no less of the ruffian." Giving the broom a couple more swipes, he added, "Remember now, Drew, what I told you about the likes of Raggy."

Drew nodded. "Yes, Jason. Thank you."

Grace was anxious to get home to see the pleased look on Mama's face. Regina could not have done as well. Perhaps now Mama would no longer call her *Gracie*.

As they walked down the hill, Grace asked Drew what he thought of the market, but his comments were vague. Sometimes Grace wished she could do things and go places with fun-loving Amy rather than glum Drew. Amy and she would have giggled and laughed throughout the entire morning.

Just as they were ready to turn the corner at Fourth and Main, she heard Drew give a groan. "Oh no," he said. "Not again."

Raggy Langler was coming toward them with a menacing scowl on his face.

"I heard you calling me a thief at the market awhile ago," Raggy said.

"I called you a thief because you are a thief," Grace returned.

"Don't make him any madder," Drew muttered, stopping in his tracks.

"So the Boston dandy goes to market with his little basket on his arm," Raggy taunted as he drew nearer. "Let's see what dapper-boy buys at the market." Bumping into Grace, Raggy grabbed at Drew's basket, yanking out the piece of muslin.

Unbalanced, Grace nearly fell, but righted herself just in time. She could only hope no eggs were broken. Raggy whipped out the cloth and draped it over his dirty hair. In a singsong voice, he said, "Oh look, I'm dressed like the dandy from Boston."

"Give that back," Grace demanded. "That's my mama's cloth. I'll call the watchman on you."

Raggy was dancing about, raising a cloud of dust beneath his feet and having a great time with his own jesting. "Now there's no big boy to save you," he taunted, waving the cloth in the air.

Grace knew the watchman who held this area was a tall, friendly man named Mr. Gedney. If only. . .

Suddenly, at the top of her voice, she began to scream as though she were dying. "Help, help, Mr. Gedney! We're being robbed!"

"Quit that caterwauling," Raggy demanded.

But Grace wouldn't stop. She screamed and hollered and yelled and stamped her feet. "Give me back that muslin!" she yelled. "You terrible, no-good thief!" Curtains rustled at windows as people peered out. Mr. Gedney came running up the hill toward them with his large rattle stick in his hand. As soon as Raggy spied him, he threw the sprigged muslin in the dirt and ran down a side street as fast as he could go.

"I'm sorry, Grace," Drew said as he picked up the cloth and shook out the dust.

"What's going on here?" Mr. Gedney demanded. He was panting heavily from his uphill sprint. "Oh, it's you, Grace Morgan. How are you, young lady?"

"Not very well, Mr. Gedney. That mean old boy tried to take our things we bought at the market."

"Come on," Drew said to Grace. "There's nothing he can do now."

"Who?" Mr. Gedney wanted to know. "What boy?"

"Raggy Langler is his name," Grace told him.

Mr. Gedney nodded. "I know him. He's the boy who lives with Mrs. Stanley."

"That's the one," Grace said. Drew was beginning to walk on down the hill. "Drew, wait for me!" she called out.

"All the watchmen from here down to the public landing have chased that boy at one time or another," Mr. Gedney told her. "But I'll keep my eye out."

"Well, he didn't really take anything, Mr. Gedney. I mean"—she tried to explain as she started walking after Drew—"he did take something, but he gave it back again."

Mr. Gedney nodded. "I'll keep an eye out just the same."

"Thank you, Mr. Gedney!" Grace called back as she ran to catch up with Drew. When she was beside him again, she asked, "Why'd you say you were sorry awhile ago? You didn't do anything."

"I know," Drew said, his eyes sad. "That's why I apologized. I didn't do anything."

CHAPTER 6

Last Day of School

Drew said good-bye to Grace at the front gate and politely thanked her for inviting him to go along. "I really did enjoy the market," he told her, "and the peppermint stick."

"You're welcome, Drew. See you tomorrow at church."

He nodded and went on his way.

When Grace presented to Mama the basket containing one cracked egg and a yard of dirty sprigged muslin, Regina said to Mama, "I knew you should never have let her go to the market alone. She's just too little."

Grace glared at the hired girl. "I am not too little. There's a boy named Raggy Langler who torments Drew terribly. He tried to take Drew's basket, and he pushed me. We saw him stealing turnips in the market."

"The boy would never have bothered you if I'd been with you," Regina put in. "Or your mama."

Sometimes Grace wished Regina didn't work for them. She could help Mama with some of the work, if only Mama would let her.

"How was it you were able to get the cloth back?" Mother asked in a kind voice. It was good to know she wasn't angry at Grace.

"Mr. Gedney, the watchman, heard me yelling and came running."

"Why didn't this bad boy named Raggy just run off with the cloth? Why did he throw it down?"

Mama's question surprised Grace. She shook her head. "Because if he kept it, Mr. Gedney would have run after him and he would have been a thief."

"But you say he stole turnips?" Mama took the items from the basket and began putting them away.

Grace didn't understand what Mama was getting at, nor did she want to know. Raggy Langler was a mean, horrible boy, and that's all there was to it. "He stole the cloth, then threw it in the dirt," she said trying to make the story worse. "He pushed me so hard that, if I'd fallen, your cabbages and turnips would have been full of dirt and the eggs all broken."

"I believe at prayers tonight, we shall pray for Raggy Langler," Mama said. "Now go to your room and freshen up. We'll have cabbage wedges with our salt pork for lunch."

Not only did Mama pray for Raggy that night, she also instructed Grace to pray for him at church the next morning. Now that was going to take some doing!

On Sundays they walked to church with Carter, Deanna, and little Matthew and Adah. Grace's bonnet was new. The ruffles and ribbons fascinated two-year-old Adah.

"Pitty ribbon," she said, wanting to touch the bonnet. Grace adored cute little Adah with her mop of copper-colored curls.

Four-year-old Matthew held tightly to Drew's hand, and Grace noted how the little boy dogged the steps of his young uncle. Carter, as usual, had little to say. Grace couldn't imagine being as quiet as Carter Ramsey. What a chore that would be! Mama and Deanna, on the other hand, always chatted nonstop.

As they entered the sanctuary, Widow Robbins was seated at the piano, playing a grand hymn. Before the piano had arrived, Grace had hated her family's second-row pew, but now she was thankful. Grace watched every move Widow Robbins made as her fingers scooted over the glossy keys, amazed at the combination of sounds that came out. Someday she would know how to create lovely music on her very own piano.

The Reverend Danforth's message lasted for several hours. Sometimes there would be a break, during which they sang hymns from the hymnbooks. If Grace had her way, they'd sing for hours and take a break to listen to a short sermon!

Although Grace only listened halfheartedly, at one point she heard the reverend say that it was God's will that all should come to repentance—that God willed no one to perish or be lost. Grace wondered, *Does that include people like Raggy and the riffraff that live in Sausage Row?* Then the Reverend Danforth added, "By our love and our example, we draw others into the kingdom."

After church, Grace thought about what those words meant. No matter how she twisted and turned them around in her head, she just couldn't see any way she could love Raggy Langler or set an example for him. She wanted to strike him and make him leave Drew alone forever.

The day of the school-commencement exercises broke sunny and bright. Grace wanted more than anything to enjoy every moment of the day, but the conversation she'd overheard the night before between Papa and Luke kept echoing in her mind. There still hadn't been a drop of rain, and the low river level meant no barges, no keelboats, and no steamboats. Grace had never seen the beautiful Ohio River so low. That in itself was scary enough.

But sitting quietly on the stair landing, she'd heard Papa and Luke talking about yet another problem—the Cincinnati banks.

"They've extended too much credit," Papa said.

"But all banks out West have operated on credit," Luke protested. "There's no other way to make it go."

"Yes," Papa answered in a low voice, "but all cities aren't suffering from lack of river traffic. It would be a double blow for us if the banks folded."

For the first time ever, Grace stopped listening and crept back into bed. What did it mean to have the banks fold? Did that mean the banknote Papa wrote for the piano would not be any good?

Grace and Amy were currently standing in front of the schoolhouse. They were in their proper position, along with hundreds of other students, waiting for the parade to begin. All of Fourth Street was decked out in bunting and banners. Grace reckoned most of the city had turned out for the occasion. It felt nice, and a little strange, to feel the warm sun on her head and face. But none of the girls wore their bonnets, and the boys had left their caps off. All the children were to be bareheaded, wear light-colored clothing, and wave streamers as they proceeded down the broad street, singing as they went.

With a pounding of the bass drum and clash of cymbals, the band struck up a lively tune and the parade was underway. Grace marched and sang and waved her streamer with all the others. At the corner of Fourth and Broadway, she saw Papa and Mama standing at the curbing with Luke and Camille. She smiled to them and waved her streamer with more enthusiasm. It was good to see Papa smiling. There had been worry lines on his brow for many weeks.

The parade led to the town square, where the children were seated on the grass. On the bandstand stood Hugh Sutton, superintendent of the city schools, who called the crowd to attention. Acting as master of ceremonies, Mr. Sutton announced the special presentations from each classroom.

When it was Grace's turn, she stood and walked proudly to the platform. The leader of the band put his pitch pipe to his lips to give her the correct key. Looking out over the thousands of faces, she searched for Mama and Papa. When at last she spied them standing beneath a sprawling oak tree, she sang to Papa the clear sweet melody of "A Mighty Fortress Is Our God." A hush fell over the crowd as the words of comfort touched fearful hearts. Coming to the second verse, she sang:

Did we in our own strength confide,
Our striving would be losing
Were not the right Man on our side,
The Man of God's own choosing.
Dost ask who that may be?
Christ Jesus, it is He;
Lord Sabaoth, His name,
From age to age the same,
And He must win the battle.

Even as she sang, Grace wondered if Jesus would help them win their battle against the awful problems of a dry river and banking systems that were falling apart. Could she be as certain as the hymn stated?

After the presentations, speeches, and prayers were completed, there were games and picnics beneath the cool shade of the trees in the square. Mama had brought Grace's school bonnet along, but no one else was wearing one, so she convinced Mama to let her run bareheaded throughout the afternoon.

She introduced Amy and Jason to her family. Jason politely invited Drew to join in the races and games with him and his friend. Grace was surprised and pleased when Drew agreed.

Amy's little sister, Leah, was a toddler near Adah's age. Amy and Grace had great fun walking among the crowds with Leah in tow. Thankfully, Raggy had not appeared that day. Nor had she seen Wesley or Karl.

As they sat in the grass near the bandstand, listening to the rousing band music, Grace mentioned the boys' absence to Amy.

Pulling Leah into her lap, Amy said, "But they're the indigent students, remember?"

"What do you mean?"

"Grace, think about it. Can you imagine their dirty clothes in the parade along with all the pretty linen dresses and the other boys' white shirts and nice bow ties? Why, they don't even have shoes!"

Grace felt silly that she'd not thought of that before. It was true. When snow was on the ground, Raggy wore a pair of boots that looked as though they'd been cast off by someone much larger than he. As soon as the frost was off, he was barefoot again. What shoes would he have worn in the parade?

Suddenly, Grace felt a little ache deep in the pit of her stomach. An ache she couldn't explain, and one that didn't want to go away.

CHAPTER 7

Drew's Challenge

Whippoorwills echoed their lonely calls in the trees above Drew's head. The dense grove of buckeye, sycamore, and honey-locust trees blocked out the dimming June sky. Only through a few patches in the leafy boughs could he see the stars beginning to come out. Beside Drew, Grace sat quietly as she stared down the bluff at the wide muddy bog that was once a rushing river. The ferries that used to carry folks back and forth from the Kentucky side to the Ohio side were landlocked and useless.

It wasn't like Grace to be still or even to sit still. Drew knew she was worried about her family. And he was worried, as well. The saddest thing to Drew was that Grace never mentioned her piano anymore. Had she lost hope?

If Drew hadn't liked Cincinnati when he first arrived, he liked it even less now. The entire city seemed to be falling apart. Land prices had caved in and factories were closing their doors. He understood some of what was happening, but most he did not.

"It's not just the lack of river traffic, is it?" he said to Grace, breaking the silence.

Grace turned to him. Her bonnet hung down her back by its ribbons. "You mean why the businesses are failing? No, Drew, it's not just the river."

Drew brushed leaves off his homespun trousers. After school let out, Deanna had found some old clothes of Carter's and cut them down for Drew. The feel of linsey-woolsey took some getting used to, but at least he would no longer be called a dandy. "I've asked Carter about things, but he won't talk."

"Same with Papa," Grace agreed. "He says I'm too young to understand. But I've heard plenty of talk between him and Luke and with Mama, too." She pulled at the tuft on a purple thistle weed. It broke apart in her hands. "I heard Papa call it a *depression*. He says now that Americans are trading with the British rather than fighting with them, British products are cheaper than our products. That puts American factories out of business."

Drew thought about that for a minute. "But the banks. . ."

"I don't understand, either. All I know is that the banknotes that *used* to be worth something aren't worth anything now."

"Carter said he was glad he didn't have any money in a worthless old bank."

"This is one time your brother may be right."

Drew looked away for fear he might see Grace cry. When she spoke again, Grace said, "Papa and Luke both trusted the bank, and now they have nothing. And the money they expected to receive from the sale of the boats won't be coming. The buyers can't come downriver to fetch them." Pulling her hankie from her apron pocket, Grace blew her nose. "Papa doesn't even know if the owners still have the money to buy the boats."

After a moment, Drew tried to change the subject. "Carter wants me to go hunting with him."

Grace brightened a bit, tucking her hankie back in her pocket.

"That's good, Drew. At least you'll be helping. I wish I could do more to help."

"I'm sort of afraid of the musket."

Grace nodded. "You can get over being afraid."

"Do you think so?" Drew sometimes envied Grace's fearlessness.

"Carter may not talk much, but I imagine he'll be a good teacher."

Drew thought about that. "He's not very patient. I mean, he's not very patient with me. He's pretty patient with Matt and Adah."

"That's because they're his own. That's different. He probably expects more of you because you're older."

"When he's gone from the house, I've been practicing splitting kindling."

"Have you?" Grace's look of surprise pleased Drew. "I'm proud of you. How're you doing?"

"Not too well, but I'm not giving up. Deanna's been helping me keep the secret."

"I've been lending a hand around the house more, too, since Mama had to let Regina go." She gave a little laugh. "I used to wish Regina didn't work for us. Now I'm sorry I had those thoughts. Regina needed the work, and Mama needed her help."

"You couldn't have known how things were going to change."

"I know, but I'm still going to be more careful about my thoughts." Methodically, she pulled the ribbons of her bonnet through her fingers. "I wish we could do more, Drew. I wish we could help somehow."

Drew knew what she meant. Now that circumstances in the city had seen a downturn, Drew felt even more guilty for eating at Carter's table. Many nights he ate only half of his portion and made sure Matthew and Adah took the rest. Then he went to bed dreaming of the heavy-laden table at his old home back in Boston. There were delicacies there, such as rhubarb pies, which he doubted he'd ever taste again. After his parents had died, it was discovered that the embargo and the war had destroyed their business. There was no money left, and strangers now lived in his Boston home.

"Come on," he said, jumping to his feet. "We're certainly not doing much good up here."

"You're right," Grace agreed as she stood and brushed dirt and leaves from her skirt, "but it's good to get away for a few moments. Even if the view does look down on a dried-up river."

They walked quietly down from the bluff together, crossing the small bridge over Deer Creek. Drew walked Grace back to her house before returning to Carter's small cabin at the edge of the woods. He filled the water bucket at the well and, heaving with all his might, carried the sloshing bucket into the kitchen for Deanna. Soon his muscles would be as strong as Carter's.

Deanna smiled and thanked him, and little Matthew came running to greet him.

"Uncle Drew," he said, "look." He held up a whistle that Drew had carved for him, which was now in two pieces. "Adah broke it," he declared. "She's a bad girl."

Adah clung to her mother's skirts, sucking two fingers of her free hand. When she heard her brother's accusations, she ducked her head.

Drew took the pieces of the whistle, "She didn't mean to break it," he said. "And I can easily make another."

Matthew began to bounce around. "Would you, Uncle Drew? Please, would you?"

"We'll look for a just-right willow branch tomorrow."

Just then, Carter appeared at the door. "Tomorrow you may be busy, little brother," he said. "Come out to the well. I want to teach you to dress out the game. Bring that sharp knife of yours."

Drew gave a little shudder as he thought of the blood and innards he was about to see. But he straightened himself, pulled his knife from his trouser pocket, and followed Carter out into the dooryard. A flickering lantern sat on the edge of the well, spreading light on the ground where Carter had placed two dead rabbits.

"Just do as I do," Carter said, lifting one of the rabbits by its hind legs. Taking his knife, he carefully made a clean slit down the midsection of the rabbit.

Drew took a quick breath and held it. Giving himself no time to think, he did the same. Within minutes, two rabbits were skinned and gutted. Drew was pretty proud of himself, and once it was over and the entrails were lying on the ground, it didn't seem half bad. Like Grace said, he could get over being afraid.

Without the fur, the rabbits looked pretty skinny. As though reading Drew's thoughts, Carter said, "They've about run all their winter fat off." Taking water from the dipper hanging on the well post, he rinsed both carcasses. "But wild game may be all that will grace our table until things change."

Drew wanted to ask questions, but he held his tongue.

Heading toward the house, Carter volunteered one more comment, "And the game is staying further and further away from all this so-called civilization."

That night's supper was salt pork and Indian corn pone, but

Deanna seemed delighted that she now had two rabbits to stew.

The next morning, Carter woke Drew early. Drew quickly dressed and ate, then helped Deanna pack their lunch of dried beef, biscuits, and water. Drew followed closely behind Carter as they made their way across Deer Creek and headed in a northeasterly direction until they were far from the noisy city.

Drew had never been in such dense wilderness, but he rather liked the solitude. Silently, Carter pointed out tracks and signs of game.

Before the day was out, Carter placed his prized musket in Drew's hands and showed him how to pour in the correct amount of powder and tamp it in. Then he demonstrated wrapping the lead ball with the cloth and tamping it down.

"This is the safety cock," Carter said, placing the percussion cap in place. "When you're ready to fire, you pull it back to full cock, then let her fly."

Drew nodded, wondering if he would falter when it came time to fire.

"Someday," Carter said softly, "I'm gonna have me a good rifle."

A few moments later, Carter pointed out a fat grouse sitting crouched beneath a bramble bush. As Drew aimed at the bird, his hands began to quiver and shake. He forced them to be still. Slowly he let the hammer fly, and the explosion slammed his shoulder. The grouse flew away unharmed.

He waited for Carter to berate him, but his brother only remarked, "Being hungry can help make you a crack shot."

It was true. When they stopped at a stream for a drink and to eat their lunch, all Drew could think of was rabbit stew! After that, he pictured food on the table every time he aimed. Late in the afternoon, he had a bead on a squirrel sitting high in a beech tree.

Slowly, slowly he let the hammer fly, and the squirrel feel to the ground with a *thud*.

Drew wanted to laugh and shout, but instead he handed the musket to Carter and ran to pick up his kill. When he came back, Carter patted his shoulder and said, "Good shot. You must be real hungry!" As they laughed together, Drew wondered why he and his brother couldn't have more moments like this.

A few days later, Drew and Grace were sent to the market to see what they could purchase. In just a few weeks the open markets in Cincinnati had totally changed. The grapes, melons, and tomatoes that Grace had promised would not be coming. No milk, cheese, or fat hens. The drought had affected the crops. Most of what little the farmers had produced, they were using themselves. And what was brought in to market often went by begging because so few people had money to make purchases.

In spite of the early hour, the air was still and hot. Under the roof of the vast market, there was only a smattering of wagons. And the produce looked pitiful. Drew was almost embarrassed to approach the farmers. Grace did a little dickering and purchased a bag of snap beans, two small heads of cabbage, and a few eggs. Before they turned for home, Drew suggested they go to Yost's.

"But we've no money for candy," she protested.

"I know, but I'd like to say hello to Jason."

Grace looked at him. "Do you think he still has a job there?"

Drew shrugged. "Let's find out."

"Let's do. If he's there, I can find out how Amy is, as well."

They hurried in the direction of Fourth Street. Inside the store, there was only one other customer. Mr. Yost hailed them as they entered. "Say there, Grace, Drew," he said with a cheery smile. "Did you come to buy me out?"

Grace chuckled at his silly remark. "I don't think we're in a position to buy you out today, Mr. Yost. We're looking for Jason. Does he still work for you?"

"Well," Mr. Yost said slowly, "he doesn't exactly work *for* me. I guess you could say he works *with* me now."

"What do you mean?" Drew asked.

Mr. Yost leaned against the counter and gave a little sigh. "When the crash hit, I had to let my workers go."

"I know how that is," Grace put in. "Papa and Luke had to do the same at the boatworks."

Mr. Yost rubbed at a scar on his face and nodded. "It's the same everywhere. In Pittsburgh and Lexington, too, I hear. Well, anyway, that Jason just wouldn't go." He chuckled as he thought about it. "Jason said, 'You can't pay me, but you can teach me. Let me stay and do what I can, and you teach me all about the mercantile business.'"

Drew nodded. He knew he liked Jason Coppock. That boy was smart.

"So," Mr. Yost went on, "he comes every day. We wait on a few customers, and then I teach him how to make orders, how to stock, and how to keep the books." He laughed again. " 'Course, there're no orders to make, so we pretend a great deal."

"So where's Jason now?" Grace asked. Drew was just ready to ask the same thing.

The light in Mr. Yost's eyes faded just a bit. "Today Jason is at home helping his family move."

"Move?" Grace asked. "Are they moving away from Cincinnati?"

"Oh, no, Gracie, they're just moving to another part of town. You see, they've lost their house."

Drew felt his stomach lurch, and he heard Grace gasp. "Oh no!" she said. "Poor Amy. Poor Mr. and Mrs. Coppock." Drew knew that Grace had been frightened her own family might lose their house after she learned that Mr. and Mrs. Chesman Billings, the richest people in Cincinnati, had lost all their holdings.

"Lots of people are losing houses and land right along with their businesses," Mr. Yost told them. "That's what happens when people live on credit. Me, I've tried to pay for everything as I go. My ma and pa taught me that long before they died." He shook his head. "But even still, we may not make it through this."

"Where'd the Coppocks move to?" Drew wanted to know.

"They found a small cabin over by Mill Creek."

"That's clear out of town!" Grace was incredulous.

"Yep," Mr. Yost answered, "and they were plenty lucky to get it."

Before Grace and Drew left, Mr. Yost held out the candy jar. "Here," he said, "each of you take one. They're getting more stale by the day." He smiled. "I promise I won't tell if you won't."

Drew hated to take something without paying, and he could see Grace felt the same way. But the shopkeeper insisted.

Soon they were carrying their basket between them, walking down the hill, sucking on their peppermint sticks.

"What are you thinking about, Drew?" Grace asked as she licked the last of the peppermint from her fingers.

They had just passed the corner where Raggy had accosted them so long ago. Drew hadn't seen Raggy for weeks. "I was just thinking," Drew answered, "that if things keep going as they are, Raggy Langler may become the best-dressed fellow in Cincinnati."

CHAPTER 8

Surprise in the Country

The Fourth of July, usually a rollicking celebration in Cincinnati, was quiet and subdued that summer. The city council voted to dispense with the great parade and instead encouraged citizens to become involved in the soup kitchens that had been set up in each part of the city. There were a few firework displays that evening, but they didn't amount to much.

Grace was disappointed. She'd looked forward to the holiday as a diversion from the gloom about her. Still, she knew the city leaders were right. How could they celebrate when people were starving?

However, a nice surprise did come a few days later. In the mail came a letter from Samantha and Owen Tate. The Tates were relatives of theirs who lived on a farm several miles north of the city. Grace wanted to open the letter right away, but Mama said they must wait until Papa came home.

It was later than usual when Papa arrived home that night. Grace wanted to show him the letter immediately, but again Mama said to wait. "Let Papa eat supper and rest his weary bones," she said. Even though Mama was tired from all the daily household chores, she still took extra care to protect Papa and make him comfortable each evening.

Finally, after their meager supper was finished, Grace brought the letter to the table. "Look, Papa. A letter from Samantha and Owen. May I open it?"

Papa smiled. "Of course you can, Gracie. Let's hope it's full of good news. I could use some."

Carefully Grace peeled open the seal and spread out the paper. She read: " 'Dear Thad, Lavina, and Gracie. . .' " Grace looked up. "When is everyone going to stop calling me that?" she asked.

"Go on," Mama insisted. "What does Samantha say?"

Grace read on:

We've heard about the hard times in the city. The drought here has been bad, as well, but we do have plenty to eat. Owen has dug the foundation for the new room on the house. We could use help in framing and finishing it.

Why don't you come for a visit and lend a hand? Have Luke and Camille come, too. It would be good to see you again. Tell Grace I have a surprise for her to see.

Love,

Samantha

Grace looked up to see Mama smiling. "A trip to the farm," Mama said softly. "That would be nice."

"And listen to this part!" Grace said. "At the bottom it says, 'Our baby is to arrive around Thanksgiving time.' "

"Oh, Thad, do you hear that? Samantha is to have her first baby! What wonderful news!"

"May we go, Papa? They need our help. You heard what she said. May we?" *A surprise!* Samantha had said there was a surprise.

Grace wondered what it could be.

"She did say they need help," Papa agreed. He leaned back in his chair. "I guess nothing here will spoil while we're gone."

Grace could hardly contain her excitement. How good it would be to have something to look forward to once again. "Papa," she said, "may we take Drew along?"

When her father paused before answering, she added, "He can work hard. Why, he's even learned to swing an ax."

"Doesn't Deanna need him there, Grace?" Mama asked.

"As Drew himself said, he's just another mouth to feed," Grace answered. "They barely have enough to eat now."

Mama and Papa looked at one another. Finally, Papa said, "Let's ask Carter. If he agrees, it's all right with me."

Grace jumped up from where she was sitting. "Please, Papa, may we take the lantern and go to Carter's house tonight?"

"Grace," Mama protested, "your papa is weary. Let him rest."

"It's all right, Lavina. Carter's gone out hunting nearly every day. I'd just as well go while he's at home." He stood up from the table. "Leave the dishes and grab your bonnet and come with us," he said to Mama.

She nodded. "It would be good to spend a little time with Deanna," she said. "Thad, would you go to the cellar and bring salt pork from our barrel? We shouldn't go empty-handed."

Grace was already running upstairs to grab her bonnet from off the hook in her room. She and Drew were going to go to the farm! Carter just had to say yes.

And Carter did say yes. His only condition was for Drew to cut extra wood for Deanna's cookstove before he left.

Carter had carried a couple of cane chairs out to the back stoop, and he and Papa sat in the warm night air, talking softly. Inside Mama played with little Adah while she chatted with Deanna. Grace and Drew ran about the clearing, helping Matt catch fireflies.

Stretched on boards at the edge of the clearing were the skins that Carter was tanning.

"This is the one I shot," Drew said, pointing to the golden brown squirrel hide. "Carter says he'll teach me to make a pair of moccasins with it. And in the fall, if I shoot a deer, he'll teach me to make leggings."

Grace noted the pride in his voice. Perhaps Drew was finally adjusting to his new home.

The next day, Papa began making arrangements for their trip. To rent a wagon for the trip, he had to write a promise to the liveryman that he would bring back produce from the farm in payment.

The morning they were to leave, Drew was at their house before daybreak. Mama made sure he ate another biscuit before they left. Mama had also packed a lunch to eat on the way, which now sat by the front door in a basket.

Luke and Papa had walked to the livery to fetch the wagon, and Grace sat on the front steps waiting. Her insides were a jumble of fluttering butterflies. It had been months since her family had been out to visit the Tate farm.

She kept wondering about the word *surprise*. Samantha had written in the letter that a baby was on the way, so that wasn't it. With a slam of the door, Drew came out carrying a buttered biscuit.

"Thank you for asking me to go along, Grace," he said.

Grace wondered if she remembered to say thank you half as

many times as Drew did. "I wanted you to go see the farm. It's ever so much fun."

"What's it like?"

"Fields of grain that seem to stretch out forever," she explained. "And a barn full of hay with cows, horses, and pigs. Oh, and there are geese, too."

"Are the geese mean?"

Grace laughed. "They're just like the pigs on the street, Drew. You take a big stick to them."

Just then, around the corner came Papa and Luke with the wagon. Harnesses jingled, and the team of sorrel horses whinnied and snuffled and bobbed their heads as Papa pulled them to a stop. "Whoa there!" he called out.

"Mercy to goodness," Mama said as she came out carrying the basket. "That's enough commotion to wake all the neighbors."

Mama was probably right. Grace was quite sure no one else in the neighborhood was up this early. The buckboard had two sets of seats up front with a long bed in back and high sideboards. Luke hopped down to help Camille up into the back seat. Grace and Drew clamored into the wagon bed. Once Mama and Papa were on board, they were off.

They took Hamilton Road north out of the city. In no time at all, they were traveling along the curving road that cut through dense stands of trees. Occasionally they came upon open farmland where acres of wheat, oats, barley, and corn had been planted. Cozy little houses snuggled into hillsides flanked by smaller smokehouses, outhouses, sheds, and at least one towering barn.

Grace had heard many times what fertile farmland their state enjoyed. And it was true. But Papa commented on the scrawny crops: "They should be a full foot taller by this time of year."

Mama replied that they should all be praying for rain.

Grace breathed in the clean fresh air and grinned at Drew. She didn't want to think about droughts, bank failures, or financial disasters. This was a holiday, and she was determined to enjoy it to the fullest.

"I hope there are baby kittens in the barn," she said.

"I like kittens," Drew said. "I had a kitten of my own in Boston."

"Your very own?"

Drew nodded. "She even stayed with me in my room."

Grace thought that would be nice. A cuddly little kitten lying on her bed. "Say," she said, "maybe that's the surprise."

"What surprise?" Drew asked.

"In Samantha's letter she said there was a surprise for me to see. Maybe it's a kitten."

Over her shoulder, Mama said, "Grace, if the surprise is a kitten, you cannot bring it home."

Grace thought for a moment. "And since I've seen kittens before, the surprise must not be a kitten."

When the warm sun was straight up in the sky, Papa stopped at a stream and allowed the horses to drink. Grace and Drew hopped down and helped spread the quilts in the grass. They opened the basket and enjoyed a picnic lunch of salt pork, slices of bread with cheese, and boiled eggs. No one commented that it wasn't a very elegant picnic lunch. It was too lovely a spot and too nice a day to complain.

Papa brought a dipper of water for the ladies, but Grace and Drew knelt down at the edge of the gurgling stream and scooped up handfuls of clear, cool water. "It's a far sight cleaner than Deer Creek," Grace said.

Just then, Drew flicked cold water on her.

"Why, you. . . !" She scooped water in her cupped palm and flung it at him, splashing him square in the face.

Drew burst out laughing and ran from her reach as she chased him through the trees. She very nearly caught him, but since he'd been spending time in the woods with Carter, he was much more agile than when she'd first met him. For the life of her, she couldn't keep up with him.

Papa's call put a stop to their game, and they came laughing and panting to the wagon. Later, Grace realized that it was the first time she'd ever heard Drew laugh—really laugh!

As dusk began to gather, the rocking of the wagon lulled Grace into a deep slumber. The next thing she knew, a loud voice called out, "Hello, hello! Welcome! We thought you'd never get here! Come on down. Owen can take care of the team. I know you're tired."

Even in her half sleep, Grace recognized Samantha's friendly voice. Rubbing her eyes, she sat up. Drew was still fast asleep on his pile of quilts. She reached over and gave him a shake. "Sleepyhead, wake up! We're here!"

Lanterns were swinging over the back of the wagon. "Well, well. If it's not our little Gracie."

That was Owen's voice. "And who is this?" he wanted to know.

Drew was sitting up and stretching.

"This is Drew," Grace said. "Carter's younger brother."

"Of course, of course. Come on, now," he said, giving them each a hand. "Samantha has a supper all laid out."

Following the soft yellow lantern light, the two went up the path to the back door. Tantalizing food aromas met them before they entered. Grace was sure nothing had ever smelled so good. There on the table were platters of frizzled ham, bowls of seasoned potatoes, and wedges of cooked cabbage. But on the sideboard was the best of all—squash pies. Grace hadn't seen a pie for ever so long.

Grace and Drew ate without talking. Grace wasn't sure if it was because she was too tired to talk or too hungry. But as she cut into her thick slice of golden squash pie, she remembered about the surprise.

"Samantha," she blurted out, "you said there was a surprise for me to see."

"And there is. There surely is," Samantha said.

"May I see it?"

"It's in the barn," Samantha explained.

"May we take the lantern out to the barn to see?"

"No surprises tonight, Gracie," Mama said firmly. "To bed with you as soon as you finish eating."

Once Grace and Drew were bedded down on quilts in corners of the kitchen, she was glad Mama had said no. Her full stomach had made her very sleepy. As she dozed off, Grace knew it wouldn't matter if there were no surprise at all. Just being at the farm was a good enough treat!

CHAPTER 9

Drew's Gifts

Early the next morning, Grace was awakened by the sounds of Samantha filling the cookstove with wood. When she looked over to wake Drew, he was gone. How could he be up before her?

"Samantha!" she said, jumping to her feet. "Where's Drew?"

"He volunteered to chop kindling for the stove." Willowy Samantha leaned down to grab another chunk of wood, shoved it in the stove, and slammed the iron door shut. Corn mush bubbled in a pot, and tall, round biscuits sat on a tin ready to go into the oven. Outside a noisy old rooster hailed the morning with his loud crowing. How could Grace have slept through all this noise?

As she hurriedly folded quilts, she asked, "He hasn't been to the barn, has he?"

Samantha laughed. "Do you think I'd let someone else see the secret first?"

Grace felt a stab of guilt. That's exactly what she'd thought. Just then Mama came in from the living room. Grace ran to give her mother a hug. Mama's face seemed free of worry lines for the first time in many days. "Mama, may I run to the barn before breakfast?"

Mama shook her head. "Breakfast first, Gracie."

Grace wanted to complain, but seeing Mama so relaxed made her keep still. She wanted nothing to ruin this perfect day.

The men were outside studying the foundation for the new room and planning the day's work. Quickly Mama, Camille, and Grace helped Samantha put breakfast on, and then they called everyone inside. Grace saw Drew's eyes brighten at the grand array of food on the table. Since there weren't enough chairs, Drew and Grace filled their plates and ate on the back stoop.

Chickens scratched about the yard. Several tall white geese strutted proudly, giving an occasional honk. The smell of the clean country air invigorated Grace and made her want to run and shout.

"I don't know which is best," Grace told Drew, "the sweet clean air or the scrumptious food."

Around a mouthful of biscuit, Drew mumbled, "Both."

Grace laughed as the boy with impeccable manners sopped gravy with his biscuit and swiped a drip off his chin with his sleeve. When his plate was clean, Drew said, "Samantha told me this morning that she's been carrying water from the well to her garden each day."

"Looks like it needs it."

"We could do that."

Grace stopped with a spoonful of mush in the air. "That's a nice thought. Between us, we can carry twice as much water as Samantha in her condition." Cleaning up the last of her bowl of mush, she jumped to her feet. "Come on, there's so much to do. And we have a surprise to see!"

"Don't tell me to come on," Drew teased. "You're the one who slept all morning."

"Slept all morning? Why, Drew Ramsey, you. . ."

She smacked at him with her spoon, but he ducked quickly into the kitchen.

When breakfast dishes were cleared, Samantha finally announced that it was time to go to the barn. Drew and Grace ran circles around Samantha, laughing and giggling as they followed the dusty path from the house to the barn. Chickens squawked and scattered from in front of the trio. Rhythmic sounds of hammering and sawing filled the air as the men framed in the new room.

Samantha chatted about how pleased she was that they'd come and how excited she was about the new bedroom. When they reached the barn, Drew helped her pull open the heavy door. Grace squinted at the dimness and inhaled the smells of leather, fresh hay, and animals. Owen's prize horses were stabled in the barn, but most of the cows and pigs were outside in the pasture.

After a moment, Grace heard faint *baa*-ing. "Sheep?" she asked, making a guess.

"Over here," Samantha said, leading to a far corner. There, in a small enclosure, were two nanny goats and three of the most darling white kid goats Grace had ever seen.

"Goats!" she exclaimed. "You have goats! Oh, Samantha, this is a wonderful surprise. Where did they come from? May we pet them?" She wanted to touch their silky fur.

Samantha reached up to get a bucket from a hook and then fetched a small stool. "An old peddler came by awhile back with these nanny goats, and it just took Owen and me one look. . . . We couldn't resist. We just had to have them. And a few weeks later, both gave birth—to these three." She gestured to the kids.

As Samantha opened the gate to the enclosure, the nearest nanny goat moved cautiously away. "Come now, Josie," Samantha cooed to the nanny. To Grace and Drew, she said, "They're not sure they trust me just yet. So you two just watch until I finish milking."

"Milking? You're going to milk them?" Grace was fascinated. Such small animals giving milk! She watched carefully as Samantha fastened the nanny's head in a stanchion to keep her still. Streams of milk echoed with a *ping-ping-ping* as they hit the tin bucket. Soon the white foam rose to the rim where Grace could see it.

"These little critters give a lot of milk," Samantha told them. She handed the full bucket to Drew. "Set that over by the door so it won't get spilled, and I'll let her loose."

Samantha unfastened the stanchion and then repeated the process with Annabelle, the other nanny. Once she was done, she opened the gate to let Drew and Grace into the enclosure. "Walk slowly now, so as not to startle them."

Grace knelt down in the hay to pet one of the kids. The coat was warm and silky to her touch. She rubbed its head and the kid pushed back. "Look, Samantha! Look how she's trying to butt."

"You're right, that is a she. A little nanny," Samantha said. "You should see them butting one another. Like three little children romping together. Cutest thing you ever saw."

"Are these ones nannies, too?" Drew asked, his arm about the necks of the other two kids.

"On your right is a billy goat, a male," Samantha replied. "The other one is a nanny."

"Will they run and play with us?" Grace wanted to know.

Samantha nodded. "They'll give you a merry chase. You'll have to keep a close eye on them."

"Let's work for a while," Drew suggested to Grace. "Then we'll come back and play with them later this afternoon."

"That's a perfect idea."

"Work? And what work will you be doing?" Samantha led the

way out and closed the small gate to the enclosure.

Drew looked at Grace as though waiting for her to speak. But she said, "You tell her. It was your idea."

His face flushed pink as he said, "We'd like to carry water to your garden while we're here."

"Why, Drew, thank you." Samantha leaned over to put her arm around him and kissed him squarely on the cheek. Now his face grew even redder. "What a relief it'll be to have a rest."

Time passed quickly as Drew and Grace carried heavy buckets of water to the rows of vegetables. The hot sun bore down on their heads. Grace found wearing her bonnet was much more comfortable than having it hanging down her back. Owen gave Drew a felt slouch hat to wear to shade his face.

They hoed weeds in the corn patch, then picked a basket of snap beans. Mama and Camille picked cucumbers and cooked up vinegar syrup to make pickles. There were carrots, turnips, and cabbages ready to be picked. Along the fence grew vines of ripening melons and pumpkins. Grace wished she lived on a farm with all this food growing everywhere. The open-air market didn't seem half so much fun. Before supper, Drew and Grace released the goats and played tirelessly about the farmyard.

The next day, Drew found several pieces of scrap lumber lying about where the men were working. Taking them to Samantha, he said, "I noticed you have no whatnot shelf in the house. I can make one from these pieces. Would you like that?"

"Drew, you'll never know how much I'd like that. Owen is able to put up a barn and drive a nail straight, but fancy work is not his cup of tea."

Drew had his trusty knife, and in the evenings, while Grace ran about playing with baby goats, Drew carved a delicately detailed whatnot shelf.

The days were passing too swiftly for Grace. She wanted this holiday to last forever. But within a week, the room was framed and finished, and there were even two glass windows hung. In the living room, Samantha's new whatnot shelf was mounted in the corner by the fireplace. Even Owen commented on what a craftsman Drew was.

The women packed foodstuffs to take home. Some would pay the liveryman, but there was still plenty to share with Carter and Deanna. There were green pickles, blackberry preserves, blocks of cheese, and baskets of goose and chicken eggs. One bag of wheat and another of corn lay in the wagon bed.

On the last afternoon, Grace and Drew sat under a leafy buckeye tree with the nannies and their kids munching grass nearby.

"Samantha says goats grow up and come fresh much quicker than a cow," Grace said.

"Come fresh?"

"Give milk."

Drew nodded. "Oh."

"And she says they eat very little, and that they'll eat most anything. They don't need a big pasture like a cow."

"I heard Samantha say that." Drew was lying on his back staring up at the cloudless sky.

"Drew, you know how we're always wishing we could do more to help out our families?"

"We do what we can. Now that I can shoot the musket and skin my own game, I feel I'm pulling my share of the load."

"What if we could do more?"

"More? How?" Drew sat up and looked at Grace. "I can tell you're thinking about something. What are you cooking up?"

"What if we could sell goat's milk?"

"It'd spoil before we got it back to Cincinnati," Drew said.

"What if we took the milk-giver with us?"

Drew smiled. "You want to take one of the nannies?"

"Yes, I want to take Annabelle." Grace smiled. "Her kid is weaned from her."

"Your mama would never allow a goat in your yard."

"A few months ago she might not. But now that there's little food and no money, she might not be so hard to convince."

Drew thought about it. "It'd be fun to have Annabelle with us," he said.

"I agree. Shall we go ask?"

"Let's go!"

First they went to find Samantha, who was out in the garden. Grace asked if she'd part with Annabelle. "I was hoping you'd ask," Samantha answered.

Mama and Camille were in the kitchen cutting up a roasting hen for supper.

As Grace expected, her mother protested. "Gracie," she said, "you don't know a thing about taking care of a goat. You're too young for that much responsibility."

"I'm not too young," Grace protested. "I can learn. We'll have milk to drink and some left over to sell."

"But you don't know how to milk a goat."

"Samantha's already taught me. There's nothing to it."

Just then, Drew spoke up. "I can build a pen and a stanchion, Aunt Lavina."

Now Mama hesitated. It was a good sign.

Then Drew added, "And I'll even help Grace take care of Annabelle."

Grace could see her mother weakening. "I suppose we could see what your papa thinks."

Papa thought it was the smartest idea he'd heard in a long time. "Fresh milk every day! Why, Lavina, who could argue with that?"

So it was settled. Owen wove a tether rope for them with a handy slipknot so Annabelle wouldn't get away from them. The next morning when they packed the wagon, the men tied Annabelle to the back.

Grace had thought she would be sad about returning to the city, but now that she had Annabelle, she was excited. Loud good-byes and thank-yous were exchanged as the wagon pulled out of the Tate farmyard. The return trip would be slower since the wagon was weighted down with supplies.

Annabelle wasn't sure she liked leaving the farm. She bleated most of the way. Mama put her hands over her ears. "Such a racket! She sounds worse than a colicky baby."

Papa answered, "You won't care about the noise when she gives buckets of milk."

Grace didn't mind the noise at all. What fun she was going to have with her new pet.

CHAPTER 10

Annabelle's Accident

The next morning, Grace and Drew were ready to launch into their milk-selling business. But while they had plenty of milk to sell, they'd forgotten one small detail. Few people had the money with which to make a purchase.

Drew had a small wagon in which to carry their crocks of milk. They walked from house to house, pulling the wagon and asking if anyone wanted to buy some milk. People sadly shook their heads and closed their doors. Grace and Drew went home discouraged.

It was Drew who came up with the idea of bartering. "No one has any money," he said, "but people have things they might want to trade."

"That's a wonderful idea," Grace agreed.

"Let's begin with Yost's Mercantile," Drew suggested. "We'll ask Deanna and Aunt Lavina what they need from the store, and then we'll ask Mr. Yost if he'll trade the items for goat's milk."

And that's just what they did. Zachariah Yost was delighted with the plan because he and his wife had two small children. At last, Grace felt she was truly being a help to her family.

When Papa learned of their plan, he commended them. To Mama he said, "Gracie and Drew make a fine business team."

Grace basked in his praise, but she still wished he'd stop calling her *Gracie*.

Annabelle's tether rope was seldom used. Grace could go nowhere but what the bleating nanny wasn't right on her heels. Grace used the rope only when she took Annabelle into town.

"That silly goat would sleep with you if she could," Mama said in exasperation.

And Grace wished Annabelle could sleep with her. The enclosure Drew built was situated in a corner of the small area behind the house, but Annabelle spent little time there. Not because the pen wasn't sufficient, but because the goat cried when no one was around. Grace had never before had a pet, and Annabelle's antics made her laugh with glee.

And laughter was sorely needed, for as the hot, dry summer wore on, conditions in the city worsened. Food supplies dwindled, and people went hungry. There weren't as many hogs roaming the streets these days. Papa heard that people were catching them and eating them. Grace knew butchering a large animal in the heat of summer meant meat that rotted quickly. People became very ill eating spoiled meat. Knowing this made her even more thankful for the small store of food they now had in the cellar.

Papa and Luke talked about another trip to the country. They planned to help other farmers with building projects in trade for food. Grace thought it was a good plan and was pleased that her papa thought of it.

For the most part, Grace had shoved the thought of her new piano far into the back of her mind. It seemed selfish to want a luxury such as a piano when people were hungry.

However, one day as she and Drew were on an errand for Mama, with Annabelle on her tether rope, Grace was again thinking about her longing for a piano.

They were coming back from Yost's Mercantile when Grace had a bright idea. "No one's in the church on a Tuesday," she said to Drew. "Let's stop in for a minute."

"Grace, you don't like the long hours at church on Sunday. Why do you want to go on a Tuesday?"

Grace studied Drew. His unruly mop of hair stuck out every which way beneath his cap. The cut-down trousers were already too short for him. Deanna had once said that Drew grew at least an inch a day. Where he used to be pale and wan, he was now ruddy and sunburned. Drew looked nothing like the dapper boy who came to them from Boston.

"I do so like church. . .at least part of church," she retorted.

"Only the music."

"Nothing wrong with that. Music holds a sermon in itself." Tugging on Annabelle's rope, she called out, "Are you coming with me or not?" The nanny, who was attempting to nibble tufts of dried grass growing at the edge of the street, bleated and gave a little leap as she scurried to follow along.

"Grace, what're you going to do?"

"The way things look, I may never have a piano of my own."

"You're not going inside the church?"

"People go into the church all the time to pray. Why can't I?"

As Drew caught up beside Grace, Annabelle gave him a playful butt on the leg. He reached down to scratch her head. "That's not exactly true," he said to Grace. "You're not going to pray, are you?"

She smiled. "I can pray while I'm looking at the piano, can't I?"

"Grace!"

"I just want to lift the cover and touch the keys. There's no reason why I can't touch it. It's not fair for Widow Robbins to be the only one allowed to play it."

"You'll have your piano someday, Grace, I just know it. Deanna always says to me, 'Let patience have her perfect work.'"

"I know. Mama quotes the same Bible verse to me all the time. And I am being patient. Very patient. But while I'm being patient, I can still look at the church piano."

They came down Walnut Street to where the stone church with its towering bell steeple loomed on a corner lot.

"What will you do with Annabelle?" Drew asked.

"You hold her and stand outside to keep watch. We'll go to the side door. There's a little grass under the tree there. Annabelle will like that."

The shade cast by the church felt good to Grace's hot feet. Here the blazing summer sun had not totally scorched the scrubby grass. "Stay on the steps," she instructed Drew. "If you see someone coming, rap hard on the door." She handed Annabelle's rope to him.

Reaching out to take it, Drew said, "I shouldn't help you get in trouble, you know."

"There'll be no trouble, Drew." She stepped up on the cool stone step. Glancing about, she saw no one. The brass knob turned easily in her hand. "I'll leave the door ajar. Remember, rap hard."

Drew nodded, then sat down on the step and let Annabelle's rope out to give her wide range of the available grass.

Inside the church, the air was cool, with a kind of musty aroma. Grace made her way past the rows of pews to where the lovely piano sat. Soft light from the window fell across the shiny wood, making it gleam. With trembling fingers, she reached for the little knobs in the front and lifted the cover. It folded back once, then lifted once more to expose all the neatly lined black-and-white keys. Nervously, she glanced over her shoulder. The sanctuary was still empty and quiet.

Her heart was fairly thudding in her throat. She spread her skirt and sat primly on the stool, then allowed herself to actually reach out and touch the keys. They were as cool and as glossy as she knew they would be. Without pressing a key, she trailed her fingers up and down the keyboard. In her mind, she saw how Widow Robbins's fingers pounded out the chords for the hymns every Sunday. She wondered if there was a lighter way to make the melodies come to life.

From the music rack, she pulled down the hymnal and fanned through the pages. If only she knew how to read the notes. Surely it wouldn't hurt to press just one key. She did so, and the sound of the note startled her. She pressed another and then another. Within a few moments, she found sets of notes that sounded pleasing together and others that grated on her ears.

A little noise sounded behind her, making her gasp. Turning around, she said, "Oh, Annabelle, it's only you."

Then she jumped from where she was sitting. From the nanny's mouth hung a partially chewed hymnal. Down on the aisle were three more that also were partially chewed.

"Annabelle! What are you doing in here?"

"And I might ask you the same thing, young lady!" There at the door stood the Widow Robbins.

Grace froze. Where was Drew? Why hadn't he rapped on the door?

Widow Robbins snapped her parasol shut and tucked it beneath her arm. With a scowl on her thin face, she walked slowly up the aisle. Her long, black silk dress made little swishing noises as she picked up bits and pieces of chewed hymnals along the way.

"Just wait until I talk to your parents about this," she said sternly, her eyes narrowing. "Not only have you broken the rules about not touching my piano, but you have allowed this mangy animal inside the house of God."

Grace stood to her full height. "Annabelle isn't mangy. And she didn't mean any harm. I didn't bring her in, she. . ." Grace stopped. She'd better not say that she'd left Drew to guard the door. Where could he be? She knelt down to take the hymnal from Annabelle and placed it on a pew. The edges were a mess. Annabelle bleated and gave Grace a gentle butt on the arm.

The widow stepped to the piano, took out her lace hankie, carefully wiped down the keys, and then quietly closed the lid. "You are never to touch this piano. Is that clear?"

"Yes, ma'am." Grace twisted the ends of Annabelle's dangling rope.

"Now take that creature and leave the premises. I'll discuss this with the Reverend Danforth, and then we'll pay a visit to your parents and discuss your actions."

"Yes, ma'am," Grace said again. She tugged at the rope and started down the aisle, then stopped. "I'm very sorry about the damage Annabelle caused. But I think more people should be allowed to use the piano," she said boldly. "After all, the church belongs to everyone."

Widow Robbins pressed the hankie to her forehead, then made scooting motions with her hand. "Go. Leave, before my anger takes over."

Out in the hot sunshine, Grace looked up and down the street for Drew. Nothing. Something had to have happened. But what?

All she knew to do was to head toward home. No sooner had she left Walnut to turn onto Second Street than Drew came running toward her from a side street.

"Hey, Grace! I almost caught him!" he called out.

"Drew Ramsey. How could you? I left you to guard the door, and you deserted your post." She stopped and waited for him to catch up. Perspiration dripped from his beet-red face. His hat was scrunched in his hand, and he was heaving great breaths. Suddenly his words registered. "Almost caught who?" Grace wanted to know.

"Why, Raggy. Who else?"

"You were chasing Raggy Langler?"

Drew beamed a wide smile. "I was."

"Why? What did he do?"

"He tried to come at me and grab Annabelle's rope. So I stood up to him and gave him a hard shove."

Grace could barely believe her ears. "Then what?"

"He tried to fight back, but I tripped him. When he started to run, I tied Annabelle to the doorknob and chased him. Almost caught him, too."

Grace shook her head. This was almost worth getting caught by Widow Robbins. She had touched the piano, and Drew had chased Raggy. Two splendid victories!

When she told Drew about Annabelle getting loose and what happened to the hymnals and about the widow coming in, he was crestfallen. "I'm sorry. Your papa will be angry with you. What do you think will happen?"

"If Raggy tried to steal Annabelle, you did the right thing.

Whatever happens will happen."

Mama was embarrassed and quite distraught following the visit from the Reverend Danforth. Papa didn't seem quite as upset as Mama, but Grace was duly scolded by both and sent to bed early that night. Mama and Papa agreed that somehow Grace would have to pay for the hymnals, no matter how long it took.

"Perhaps I can find people who will pay cash for Annabelle's milk," Grace said solemnly. "Then I'll be able to pay the debt." But the thought made Grace feel bad since she'd hoped to use the milk to help Mama and Papa.

Sitting on the edge of her small rope bed, she gazed out the window, wishing she were outside playing because it was cooler. Only a slight breeze ruffled the treetops, and it was stuffy and hot in her bedroom.

The thought of Drew chasing Raggy through the streets amazed Grace. When she had asked him what he would have done if he'd caught Raggy, Drew had said he didn't know. With Raggy's larger size, he could whip Drew. But Drew had saved Annabelle. If Raggy had stolen the nanny, he'd probably be having her for supper right about now.

Grace was sorry the hymnals had been chewed up, because she loved the fine songbooks their church owned. But she'd never be sorry she touched those lovely ivory keys. Closing her eyes, she made herself remember how they felt beneath her fingers. *Let patience have her perfect work.* Waiting was so hard, how could it be a "perfect" work?

CHAPTER 11

The Storm

Because of Annabelle's size, Grace had a hard time leading her around. When Drew wasn't with Grace, Annabelle nearly dragged Grace by the tether. But when left in her enclosure, the goat made such a racket that the neighbors complained. Grace lived on a crowded street where the houses were close together. The offer of goat's milk did nothing to appease the disgruntled neighbors.

"We need our sleep," said Mr. McClarren, who lived directly behind them. Mrs. McClarren had five little ones to take care of, and she heartily agreed.

There was nothing to do but let Drew take Annabelle to his house. In the clearing near the banks of Deer Creek, there were fewer houses nearby. Drew dismantled the enclosure and used the rough planks of lumber to construct a new one behind the Ramsey home.

Even though she knew it was for the best, Grace was sad to have to part with Annabelle. Of course, she'd see the goat often, but it wasn't the same as having her right outside the back door.

Both Matthew and Adah were delighted to have Annabelle at their house and squealed with delight when she licked their hands.

Being nearer the woods turned out to be much better for Annabelle. She could be tethered among the trees far from the house, where she could eat grass and weeds to her heart's content.

It was a muggy, still day in late August when Drew and Grace decided to go for a trek up past the bluff and take Annabelle with them. The city was hot and depressing. Grace had never seen Papa so sad. He'd had some work to do in the country helping farmers with building projects, but not enough to support their family. The drought had ruined the gardens and fields of most farms in the area.

Although Carter continued hunting, he often came home empty-handed. The drought had driven the small game deeper into the dense forests and up into the hills, where spring water sustained them.

When Grace and Drew took Annabelle up into the woods, Grace could forget the awful problems. On this day as they started out, little Matthew put up a terrible squall to go along. Usually Deanna distracted him or talked him out of it. But for once, Deanna seemed unable to cope.

"Perhaps this one time," she said, looking at Grace and Drew with tired, pleading eyes.

Grace knew that short-legged Matthew would slow them down and keeping an eye on him would be a worry. Taking Annabelle was problem enough. But how could they say no?

"All right," Drew said. Grace was glad he was the first to answer. "Come along." He reached out his hand, and Matthew ran to grab it.

Down through the dry creek bed they went, Annabelle bleating with joy at every step. Since following the creek bed was easier than walking through dry, prickly underbrush, they followed it awhile, then made their way up the other side to higher ground.

Usually the woods were much cooler, but today the heat penetrated through the green canopy of tall trees.

Grace sang songs as they walked along. Matthew loved the boatmen songs and asked for them over and over. Usually Grace could sing them all and never get tired, but today the air was so heavy, it was as though she couldn't get her breath. After an hour or so, they came to a clearing, and she suggested they tether Annabelle and sit down.

"Annabelle sure is producing milk," Drew said. "How long do you think it will last?" He pulled out the canteen he'd filled with well water and handed it to Grace.

"I'm not sure. I'll have to ask Samantha." She took a swallow of the warm water and let it trickle down her dry throat. Matthew was fascinated with the way Annabelle cropped the grass. He sat close by the goat, watching her every move.

Drew took back the canteen and offered it to Matt. "Just a few swallows, Matt," he said. "We need it to last till we get back."

Matt nodded and tipped the canteen carefully.

Grace loosened the strings of her bonnet. "I believe this has been the longest summer of my life." Sprawled out on the grass, she was painfully aware of how short her dress was becoming. She'd grown a few inches during the summer just as Drew had. But there'd be no new dresses for school.

Matt looked up from watching Annabelle. "What's that noise?"

Grace sat very still for a moment. "It's rumbling."

"Could it be. . . ?" Drew asked.

"Thunder?" Grace queried, jumping to her feet.

They couldn't see the horizon through the dense trees. The sky above them was still sunny and hazy blue.

"Let's go look!" Grace pulled up the tether stick and pulled on Annabelle, who wasn't ready to leave this lush pasture.

Drew came from behind and gave the goat a shove just as another rumble sounded. "It is, Grace! It's thunder! I bet it's going to rain. And when it rains, the river will be up—"

"Hurry!" Grace interrupted with panic growing in her voice. "We've got to get home!"

"Why? It's just rain. I want to be in the rain."

"I should have known from the heavy, still air," Grace said, pulling on the goat's rope as hard as she could and heading quickly back the way they came. "It gets still like that before a bad storm. Papa's warned me, but I forgot. It hasn't rained for so long."

"I'm scared," Matt said.

"Maybe we could find a cave," Drew suggested, taking hold of the younger boy's hand and hurrying his step. "Carter says there're lots of caves out here."

"If we happen upon a cave, we'll sure crawl inside, but it's foolish to try to hunt for one."

Just then the crashing sound of thunder echoed above their heads and a cool wind swished through the tops of the trees. Annabelle bolted, and Grace nearly tumbled as she tried to follow.

"It's almost on us!" Grace called out.

Matthew began to cry, so Drew stopped to take him up piggyback. This slowed him some, while Annabelle dragged Grace on ahead. They were about halfway back to Deer Creek when they could see greenish-gray clouds boiling up in the west. Grace felt two fat raindrops hit her face. So long they'd prayed for rain, and now it had arrived in a furious storm. It just didn't seem fair.

"See that big tree?" Drew called out. Rain was falling in gray sheets. "Let's get under there and stay!"

"Let's do!" Grace answered. She pulled and tugged on the rope as Annabelle kicked up her heels and bleated out her misery and fright. The sunlight was gone, and even though it was early afternoon, it was dim as dusk.

"I want my mama!" Matthew cried as Drew set him down beneath the tree.

Grace wished Matt were back with his mama, but she didn't say so. After all, her own mama would be worried, as well. Thunder crashed about them like giant cymbals from the marching band. It felt good to have the hard, pelting rain out of their faces. Grace's petticoats clung to her ankles. She put her arms about Annabelle's neck and tried to calm the frightened goat.

"I just remembered, Drew," Grace said. "Papa said never to stay under a tree in a thunderstorm."

"Carter said something like that to me, too," Drew agreed. "But it's so bad right now we have no choice. We need to watch out for Matt."

"Take me home," Matthew whined as he rubbed his eyes with his fists.

Just then a clap of thunder caused Annabelle to leap in the air, and the wet rope slipped from Grace's grasp.

"Oh no!" she cried. "Annabelle, come back! Drew, help!"

Quickly Drew heaved Matthew up on his back. "Follow her, Grace! We're right behind you!"

Sliding on the wet leaves, Grace sped out in the direction Annabelle had taken. Thankfully, it was toward home.

The three had not gone more than a few yards when a blinding flash of light filled the air around them and a crash sounded so loud it made Grace's ears ache. She turned to look and was aghast to see that the fierce lightning had sent the massive tree they had just been sitting under crashing to the ground.

Drew stopped, as well. They were numb with shock.

"Drew," Grace said, "I think Annabelle just saved our lives."

"She did that, all right." He adjusted the weight of the whimpering Matthew. "Hush now, Matt. It's all right. We're headed home." Then he laughed out loud. "Home," he repeated, "where Annabelle will probably be waiting for us as if nothing had happened."

Grace joined in the laughter, but her voice was all quivery. She couldn't wait to hug Annabelle's neck. The rain had lessened some and the wind had calmed. By the time they reached Deer Creek, water was rushing freely down the creek bed. No more walking in the dry bed. They made their way to the rickety old bridge and crossed there.

The sight of flowing water thrilled Grace. Maybe this meant there'd be river traffic soon.

Annabelle was indeed waiting in the dooryard of the Ramseys'. Deanna's look of relief when she met the three drenched children at the door told them how worried she'd been. She stoked up the cookstove and made them stand by it until they stopped shivering. Cups of hot cider helped take the chill off.

"Earlier today, I never thought I'd be cool again," Grace said between chattering teeth. "Now look at me."

Deanna offered to let Grace put on one of her old dresses, but Grace insisted that she go on home so Mama wouldn't worry. But first they told Deanna the story of how Annabelle saved their lives. Even Matt helped add a few vivid details.

"*Boom!*" he said, flinging his hands in the air. "The big old tree went *boom* and fell down."

"If you hadn't chased after the goat. . ." Deanna shook her head and bit her lower lip. "God watches after His own," she said. Her voice trembled as she spoke.

The welcome rains fell off and on for a number of days, until finally one morning Grace heard the most beautiful sound. The melodious tones of a keeler blowing his tin horn echoed through the valley. She was eating breakfast when she first heard it.

She gobbled down her food and told Mama she was going to Drew's to help with Annabelle. By the time she reached Drew's house, Annabelle had been fed and was tethered at the edge of the clearing.

"Drew," Grace said, "did you hear the horn?"

He nodded. "I did. At least the barges and keelboats can get through."

"Let's go see."

"See what?"

"The boats come in, silly."

"From the bluff?"

Grace shook her head. "From the landing."

"But your mama won't like that. We can watch from the bluff."

"From the bluff we can see them come downriver, but only on the landing can we see them unload." She started out as though she expected him to follow. "It's been forever since a boat unloaded, and I don't want to miss it."

She could tell he was thinking about it, but in a moment he was by her side. "I hope we don't get into trouble," he said.

"We'll watch the boats from the landing just for a little while. Then we'll come back and help Deanna with her chores."

Sure enough, three keelboats were at the landing. One was larger than the rest, with space for eight rowers for traveling upstream. This keelboat had a large, boxy cabin in the center where passengers could get shelter from the weather.

Grace led Drew to an opening between a warehouse and the saddlery where they could see but not be seen. She made sure they stayed on the other side of the landing from the boatworks just in case Papa and Luke might be around. However, since work had come to a complete standstill, the men seldom came to the landing anymore.

From the talk on the landing, Grace and Drew learned that these boats had come up from St. Louis just as soon as the rains began.

Suddenly Grace gave a gasp. Emerging from the cabin of the larger boat was a lovely lady dressed in a fine traveling frock the color of moss in the woods. Her bonnet was lined with ruffles, and the bow was tied smartly beneath her proud chin. Long gloves graced her slender arms up to her elbows. She looked as though she'd stepped out of a fashion catalog from Yost's Mercantile rather than from the cabin of a boat. Grace could only stare, her mouth gaping.

CHAPTER 12

Sadie Rose

"Drew, do you see that lady?" Grace asked in a whisper.

She looked over at Drew, who was bug-eyed, as well. "I'm not blind," he said. "What do you suppose she's doing coming here? There's nothing in Cincinnati."

They waited a minute to see if a gentleman came to her side. A small crowd was gathering on the landing. The news had traveled that a trickle of river traffic had begun. Perhaps someone would soon come down to meet the well-dressed lady.

"Do you suppose she's traveling alone?" Grace whispered.

Drew shook his head. "Impossible."

But the lady, with her head erect, proceeded to lift the skirt of her empire dress and walk across the running board of the boat to the gangplank.

"Maybe it's not so impossible," Grace said. "She may have a good deal of money and she may need help with her bags." Pulling Drew's sleeve, she said, "Follow me. Hurry."

"Grace, we can't. . . ."

"Then I'm going alone, and I'll have all the coins to myself."

Pushing through the crowd, she sensed Drew was on her heels. Boldly Grace walked right up to the lady. Up close she was even lovelier, with cheeks as smooth and rosy as a fresh peach. Grace could see she wore "paint" on her lips, making them redder than they really were. She'd heard stories about painted ladies. A little shiver ran up her spine.

"Hello, ma'am," Grace said, suddenly wishing her dress were not so small and faded. "Welcome to Cincinnati. My name's Grace Morgan. My father builds boats over at the boatworks down there." She waved toward the far end of the landing. Grace didn't want this fine lady to think she was some waif from Sausage Row.

A smile made the picture-perfect face come alive beneath the delicate bonnet. "Well, good morning to you, Grace. And who might this be?" She motioned to Drew, who stood at Grace's elbow.

"Oh, this is Drew Ramsey, my cousin. He's my friend, too. You can call him Drew."

The lady adjusted her ruffled parasol and held out a dainty gloved hand. "Drew, Grace. My name is Sadie Rose. I'm honored to make your acquaintance."

"Sadie Rose," Grace said softly. "That's a beautiful name. Sadie Rose what?"

"Just Sadie Rose. It's enough, don't you think?"

"Oh, yes, ma'am. It's perfect," Grace replied. Why, Sadie Rose even smelled like roses. "Where are you headed?" Grace asked, suddenly remembering her mission.

"I'm going to stay at Kingsley's boardinghouse."

"Drew and I know right where that is. We can show you the way and carry your bags, as well."

Again came the smile that seemed to light up the entire landing. "That's a kind offer," said Sadie Rose. She gave her reticule a little shake. Grace could hear coins jingling. "Of course, I'd make it worth your while. Wait here while I see about having my trunk carried up later."

Since the streets were still fairly muddy, Grace deemed it best that they take Sadie Rose up Lawrence Street, which was not quite as steep as the others.

The bags were heavy, and before they were halfway to the boardinghouse, Grace and Drew were puffing.

"I hope it's not too much for you," Sadie Rose said.

"Oh no, ma'am, not at all. Drew and I like to work. We work all the time. That is, we would work all the time if there were more work to do."

"I've heard your city has suffered hard times this summer."

"You heard the truth," Drew put in.

"How long are you staying?" Grace asked between breaths.

Sadie Rose paused. "I'm undecided just now," she said.

Grace knew it was rude to ask too many questions, but she couldn't help herself. She wanted to know everything about this lady. "How did you travel all that way by yourself with those ornery boatmen?" she asked.

"I paid for protection."

Grace gave a little chuckle. "That's a smart plan."

Drew wasn't so sure. "I've heard of boatmen who've killed their passengers just to get the money," he said.

Sadie Rose stopped and looked at Drew. "Those passengers were probably snooty dandies from back East who thought they were better than those of us out West. You have to understand the boatmen in order to get along with them."

Grace saw Drew's ears turn pink. He used to think anyone on this side of the Allegheny Mountains was some kind of mindless ruffian. But he was learning differently.

"Mrs. Kingsley's boardinghouse sits at the end of this block, Miss Sadie Rose."

"Good. And you can just call me Sadie Rose. Plain and simple."

"Yes, ma'am, Sadie Rose," Grace answered.

At the front porch of the boardinghouse, Drew and Grace struggled to get the heavy bags up the steps. Once they did, Sadie Rose pulled open the reticule and placed two coins in each upturned palm. Grace hadn't seen a coin for many months. It felt cool and solid in her fist. She looked at Drew and smiled. Now she could pay for the damaged hymnals at the church.

"May we show you anything else in town, Sadie Rose?" Grace wanted to know. "After you've unpacked and settled in?"

"Why, yes. Do you know a man by the name of Eleazar Dunne?"

Grace felt Drew looking at her. "Yes, ma'am, I surely do. And I can take you right to the door of his place." Drew nudged her in the side with his elbow. She ignored him. "We'll be right here on the steps waiting for you, Sadie Rose."

"Thank you, children," replied the melodious voice. "How kind you are to a stranger."

Just then, the portly Mrs. Kingsley appeared at the door, wiping her hands on her apron. "Ain't takin' no boarders, 'less you got real money," she said curtly. "No credit."

"Good morning, Mrs. Kingsley," Grace said, stepping forward.

"Well, morning, Gracie. What are you doing around here?"

Ignoring the question, Grace introduced Sadie Rose and assured the matron that Sadie Rose was good for the rent money.

Mrs. Kingsley squinted at the immaculately dressed lady standing on her porch. "Very well, I'll take your word for it, Grace." She pushed the door open farther and stepped back to let Sadie Rose inside.

When the women were out of earshot, Drew said, "Grace Morgan, have you gone daft? We can't take her to a tavern! Especially a tavern on Front Street! Your mama will tan your hide and hang it up to dry if she ever finds out."

"If she ever finds out. But she won't. And this money can pay for new hymnals at the church. And maybe even a little food, if there's any food left in the city to buy." Grace sat down on the top step of the porch to wait. "These are desperate times, Drew. Desperate times call for desperate measures."

Once she'd said the words, she was pleased at how grown-up it sounded. Maybe when she handed the money to Mama, she could say, "Now, please don't call me *Gracie* again." But how was she going to explain the money without telling the story? She'd have to think of something.

Drew, she could tell, was still stewing about going to a tavern on Front Street, but Grace pretended not to notice. Presently, Sadie Rose came back out the door. Gone was the moss green traveling dress with matching jacket. Now there was a beautiful afternoon dress of the finest raspberry-colored taffeta Grace had ever seen.

Jumping to her feet, Grace said, "Sadie Rose, you're so beautiful!"

Sadie Rose just smiled. "Thank you, Grace. Now, shall we be on our way?"

"I've never heard of a lady traveling alone on a keelboat, and I never heard of a lady going alone to a tavern," Grace said. "What will you do there?"

Sadie Rose's lilting laughter bubbled like a little stream up in the hills. "By my leave, Grace, you're about the most curious girl

I've ever met. If you must know, I'm the new singer and piano player for Mr. Dunne."

Grace felt her heart pick up a beat. She glanced over at Drew, whose eyebrows were raised. "You know how to play the piano?" Grace asked.

"Been playing since I was knee high to a mosquito."

"And you sing?"

"Like a bird."

"Grace sings," Drew said, hardly able to keep out of this conversation.

"Does she now?"

"Oh, Drew," Grace said, but inwardly she was glad he'd told Sadie Rose.

"Yes, ma'am," Drew went on. "Last May she was chosen to sing at school commencement."

Last May seemed like such a long time ago to Grace. The long, hot summer had not been fun at all.

"If you're such a good singer," said Sadie Rose, twirling her parasol, "let's hear you sing something."

Grace never had to be asked twice. She burst out in a lively boatmen song. On the chorus, Sadie Rose joined in but moved a couple of notes higher to harmonize perfectly.

When the song was over, Sadie Rose said, "Your cousin was right, Grace. You do sing well."

"Thank you, Sadie Rose. Your voice is like an angel's."

"An angel I am not, but I thank you kindly for the sentiment."

"Right down there is Dunne's Tavern," Grace said, pointing down Front Street.

"I see the sign," said Sadie Rose. "You two can run on now."

Again Grace heard the lovely *clink* of coins. This time Sadie Rose handed each cousin a single coin. Now Grace had three. She could hardly believe it.

"But you can't stay in this area alone," Drew insisted. "Don't you want us to walk you back?"

Sadie Rose touched Drew's shoulder lightly with her gloved hand. "Young Drew, what a gentleman you are. Thank you, but I need your help no longer today. Mr. Dunne will see to my safe journey back to the boardinghouse."

Grace knew Sadie Rose would be singing at the tavern until the wee hours of the morning. Even in the worst of times, there still seemed to be business at the taverns, especially those down on Front Street. Papa said when times got hard, men either prayed or drank. Grace was thankful her papa prayed.

As she and Drew trudged back through the muddy streets toward home, Grace could hardly keep still. She wanted to laugh and sing and shout. What a splendid day it had turned out to be!

"I can hardly believe such a fine lady would sing at a tavern," Drew was saying.

"There's nothing wrong with singing at a tavern," Grace said in defense of her new friend. But she wasn't sure she was right. She'd heard stories about men fighting and killing one another after becoming drunk at a tavern. One thing she knew for sure—Sadie Rose was a very nice lady.

As she and Drew passed through the edge of Sausage Row, the smells were awful. Sewage and garbage lined the streets. Houses were little more than shacks, nothing like the fine brick home Grace's papa had built for his family. Vacant buildings with boarded-up windows bore testimony of the hard times in the city.

"I suppose we should have gone up to Second Street," Drew said, wrinkling his nose.

Grace silently agreed. Although there might be garbage in other parts of the city, nothing ever smelled as bad as Sausage Row. In her apron pocket were her three coins. She held them tightly in her fist and kept her hand in the pocket.

"What are you going to tell your mama about the money?" Drew asked.

He must have been reading her thoughts. She was wondering the same thing. "Why, I'll just tell her the truth. That a boat came in, we went to watch, and then we carried bags for a passenger."

Drew nodded. "I guess that sounds fine, but she doesn't like you going to the landing."

"Perhaps the sight of money will make it all right. What will you tell Carter and Deanna?"

"Carter has never forbidden me to go to the landing. . . ."

Just then, a terrible ruckus in an alleyway behind the vacant buildings broke into their conversation.

"Give that back!" they heard a voice yell. "That's mine. Give it back!"

"Someone's in trouble," Grace said.

"Stay out of it, Grace." Drew tugged on her arm, but she pulled away.

"That voice sounds like Raggy." She stopped to listen. "We've got to do something, Drew. Follow me."

CHAPTER 13

A Visit with Amy

Grace backtracked and made her way carefully around a vacant warehouse, hoping Drew was right behind her. Peeking around the corner, she saw two boys, bigger than Raggy, who were taunting him. She motioned for Drew to come beside her and look.

"You stay here," she said softly. "I'm going around the other way. When I give the signal, dive for their knees."

When she arrived at the opposite corner of the building, she could see the boys had something that Raggy desperately wanted. Strangely enough, it appeared to be a piece of blue flowered cloth.

"Rag–gee, Rag–gee," the boys taunted. "Carries his rag with him wherever he goes." The taller boy waved the cloth in front of Raggy like a flag. Just as Raggy leaped to grab it, the boy passed it off to his friend. There were tears in Raggy's eyes.

When Grace saw Drew peek his head around the corner, she waved her hand. The two of them ran, each one toward one of the tormenters, and slammed as hard as they could into the back of the boys' knees with their shoulders. Both boys tumbled to the ground. In a flash, Raggy grabbed the cloth and fled, disappearing around the corner of the building.

"Why, you yellow-bellied little twerps," one boy growled as

he struggled to his feet. "I'll grind you to bits and feed you to the crows."

"Come on, Drew," Grace said. "Let's get out of here." But she was quickly and roughly grabbed from behind.

"Not so quick, little girl," the second boy said. "You're gonna pay for buttin' in where you ain't welcome."

"Pay?" Grace said. Reaching into her pocket, she pulled out two of her precious coins. "Look here," she said. "I'll pay."

"Money!" the first boy exclaimed. "She has real money!"

"And it's all yours!" Grace yelled as she flung the coins as far as she could.

Immediately she was released. While the boys scrambled to retrieve the money, she and Drew made their getaway, leaving Sausage Row far behind.

When they were in their own safe neighborhood once again, they slowed their pace. Still heaving to catch his breath, Drew handed Grace two of his three coins and said, "Here, Grace. I want you to have these."

She pushed his hand away and shook her head. "You earned that money fair and square. In fact, I want you to take my last one and keep it, too. There's not enough to pay for the hymnals anyway."

Drew solemnly took the coin. "I'll keep it for you, but it's still yours."

Grace nodded.

They walked along in silence for a time. Then Drew ventured to say, "I thought you didn't like Raggy Langler, but you helped him. That doesn't make much sense to me."

"I guess I just don't like to see bullies win, no matter who the bullies are."

That night at supper, Papa seemed in better spirits than he'd been for many weeks. "With a few keelboats getting through, perhaps trade will begin to pick up," he said. "We'll pray the fall rains come early and are plentiful. Before you know it, the landing could be booming once again."

Mama had cooked up a kettle of the dried beans Papa had brought back from one of the farmers for whom he'd worked. At least it was a change from the steady diet of salt pork and corn-bread. Grace noticed that Papa was always careful to say a blessing over their meals, no matter how little they had.

As they were eating, Mama shared her good news, as well. A letter had arrived from Samantha saying she and Owen would be coming for a visit and would bring as many provisions as they could. "Eggs and cheese," Mama said, closing her eyes. "How good that will taste. Maybe watermelon. *Mmm.*"

Later that night, Grace lay tossing about in her bed. The hot August night made sleeping difficult. Not a bit of breeze fluttered through her dormer windows. Grace couldn't seem to get the look of Raggy's sad face from her mind. It was a puzzle. Why would Raggy Langler fight two bigger boys for a little piece of flowered cloth? Although she still didn't trust Raggy, suddenly he didn't seem like such a threat anymore.

A couple of times during the summer, Grace had received permis-sion from Mama to walk to Amy's house, or rather to the cabin where the Coppocks now lived. Since it was situated far on the west side of town, Mama didn't like Grace to go there alone. But when

Drew could go along, Mama was more willing.

Even though Grace loved Amy, it made her sad to visit the small cabin and see that the family didn't have many of the nice things they used to have. Mr. Coppock had owned a lot of land, and when prices plummeted, suddenly he lost not only his money in the bank, but the land, as well.

On this day, Grace and Drew were taking a bag of dried beans to the family. The streets were once again thick layers of powdery dust, and the sun bore down hotter than ever. Perhaps Papa's prediction for early fall rain was overly hopeful.

On the way across town, Grace insisted they go by the boardinghouse in hopes of seeing Sadie Rose. Grace desperately wanted to see her new friend once again. She bravely knocked on the front door and asked to see Sadie Rose, but Mrs. Kingsley glared at her sternly.

"There'd be no reason for a girl like you to visit with the likes of Sadie Rose, Gracie. You can't see her anyway because she's asleep. She sleeps most of the day. Every day. Even Sundays!" With that, she closed the door.

Grace was indignant. "The likes of Sadie Rose," she muttered as they walked away. "What a terrible way to talk."

"She didn't mean anything by it," Drew replied. "Remember, Grace, most people don't approve of ladies who spend time in a tavern."

"But Sadie Rose is different."

"From what?"

Grace shrugged. After all, what did she know about ladies in taverns? "I don't know. She's just different, that's all."

Thankfully, Drew didn't argue. He never did.

The Coppocks' cabin sat in a clearing near Mill Creek. Amy

was sitting under a shade tree in the front yard, watching her new baby sister and sewing a patch on a pair of Jason's trousers. Her little sister Leah played in the dirt nearby.

A smile lit her face when she saw the pair approaching. Jumping up, she ran to give Grace a hug. "How good to see you again! I miss you awfully." After grabbing up the baby and taking Leah's hand, she led them inside.

Mrs. Coppock greeted Drew and Grace graciously and offered to fix them each a cup of dandelion tea. Though Grace didn't care for dandelion tea, she didn't want to be rude, so she said yes.

Grace wished she and Amy could visit alone like old times at school. If only their families attended the same church, at least she'd see her friend on Sundays. Grace wanted to tell her about Sadie Rose and describe her fashionable frocks and bonnets. She wanted to tell her about seeing Raggy crying over a little piece of flowered cloth.

But a private conversation was impossible. As usual, the visit would be short. Mrs. Coppock was grateful for the beans, but Grace could tell it was an embarrassment to the woman to accept them and to Amy, as well. They had had so much, and now they had virtually nothing. The very thought made Grace's heart ache.

Later that afternoon at Drew's house, he showed Grace the stanchion he'd constructed. "See how it works?" He demonstrated by moving back and forth the slant that would hold Annabelle's head firm as she was milked. They'd been tying Annabelle's head close to a post when they milked her, but the goat moved around more than they'd like.

"Let's try it out," Grace suggested.

Together they went to the edge of the clearing. Drew lifted the tether out of the ground, and they led the goat to the stanchion. It was a perfect fit.

"Get a bucket," Grace instructed.

Drew did so and also brought her the T-shaped stool he'd made. Grace situated herself beside the goat, just as she'd done for weeks. She firmly grasped the teats and began to pull. "Drew, it works like a charm!"

Streams of milk flowed into the bucket as Annabelle stood still. For once, they weren't losing quarts of milk because of Annabelle's hooves bumping the bucket. Even quiet Drew grew excited.

"Deanna," he called out, "come and see! The stanchion works!"

After Deanna and the children had watched Grace and Drew take turns milking Annabelle, Grace turned to Deanna and asked, "Annabelle is giving so much milk; do you think we could make some goat's cheese?"

"What a fine idea," Deanna said. "I know just where my cheese-cloths and wheels are packed away."

"Deanna!" Grace called as the young woman turned toward the house.

"Yes?" Deanna asked.

"Could we keep this a secret from my parents? I'd like to surprise them."

Deanna smiled. "Of course, Grace. Now let's get to work."

Several days later, the cheese-making process was complete. Grace insisted that Deanna keep part of it for her own family. Deanna wrapped the remainder of the cheese in some cloth and placed it in a stone jar for Grace to carry home.

Later, when Mama and Papa tasted the soft cheese spread on some cornbread, Grace studied their faces.

"Mmm," Papa said as he set his cornbread down. "That's about the best cheese I've ever tasted in my life. What do you think, Lavina?"

Grace was surprised to see tears brimming in Mama's eyes. "I do believe Gracie is growing up, Thad. It's a big job to care for a goat, then milk her and make cheese, as well."

What beautiful words to Grace's ears. She ran to Mama's side and gave her a hearty hug.

A few days later, the Tates' buckboard came rumbling up the street in front of the Morgan home, and Grace ran out the front door to greet them.

Their wagon was laden with bags and barrels. A wicker basket held a fat watermelon, along with a few cucumbers, carrots, and turnips. In a crate were two cackling chickens. Thoughts of tasty chicken and dumplings made Grace's mouth water. Finally, something to eat other than salt pork!

CHAPTER 14

A Summer Feast

"Annabelle's giving lots of milk!" Grace cried out as she ran around to Samantha's side of the wagon. "We've even made cheese."

Owen secured the brake on the wagon. Laughing, he said, "Well, well. Hello to you, Grace. Good to see you."

"Grace Morgan," Mama corrected, "what an improper greeting." To Owen and Samantha she said, "I dare say this child has totally lost all decorum this summer. Everything has been at loose ends."

"Please, Lavina," Samantha said, "don't apologize. We love Grace's exuberance." She patted her large tummy. "I hope our little one is made of the same cloth."

Owen jumped down and came around to assist his wife. While Papa helped Owen unload the wagons, the women went inside to catch up on all the latest news.

Luke and Camille, as well as Carter, Deanna, and the children, were invited for Sunday dinner. It would be a celebration. A summer feast! Grace was ecstatic.

Later that evening, Samantha went along with Grace to Drew's house. When they arrived, Drew had just brought the goat in from her tether. Deanna and the children came out to greet Samantha, and together they all went out back so Samantha could see Annabelle.

Samantha could hardly believe how well the goat looked. "I

don't believe Josie is this big," she said, petting Annabelle's head and rubbing her ears. "You've taken such good care of her, Grace. I'm so proud of you."

"Mama didn't think I could do it," Grace said, stretching to stand a little taller.

Samantha nodded. "Sometimes mamas are the last ones to realize their babies are growing up." She smiled. "I'll probably be the same way."

"But I didn't do it all by myself." Grace reached out and grabbed Drew's arm, pulling him forward from where he'd been standing behind them. "Drew helped a lot."

"I'm guessing he built the enclosure and the stanchion."

"You guessed right," Grace said.

Samantha ran her hands over the wooden stanchion. "What splendid workmanship," she said.

Deanna agreed. "Drew's a good worker, and he's a gifted carpenter."

Then they all laughed as Drew blushed and ducked his head.

On Saturday, Owen wanted to see the steamboats, so the men left to go to the boatworks. The women butchered chickens and set them to boiling. Pies were baked and turnips stewed. The kitchen was unbearably hot, but no one seemed to mind.

Seeing and smelling all the scrumptious food made Grace think about Amy in her crowded cabin. How she wished Amy and her family could share in this feast. The more she thought about it, the better she liked the idea. But since this was a family gathering, she wasn't at all sure Mama would agree.

Mama, however, did agree. "Why, Gracie, what a kind heart you have," she said. Mama dumped a basket of dried apples into an iron kettle of boiling water. Later those sweet apples would be the filling for a juicy apple pie. Setting the basket down, Mama said, "We have more than enough food for the Coppocks to join us. You and Drew run over to Amy's and extend the invitation."

"Drew's gone off with Carter, Mama. But I can go by myself."

Mama hesitated. She reached up to take her large stirring spoon down from its hook and stirred the apples thoughtfully.

"If I don't go, how will they ever know they're invited?" Grace reasoned.

"I suppose you're right."

Grace's heart skipped a beat. At last Mama was beginning to trust her. "I'll fetch my bonnet," she said.

"Tell them we'll expect them at three," Mama said.

"I'll tell them." Grabbing her bonnet and tying it beneath her chin, she said, "I'll be back before supper."

"See that you are," Mama answered. "Don't dillydally."

The look on Mrs. Coppock's face when Grace offered the invitation was a sight to behold. Amy, too, fairly fluttered with excitement.

"There's plenty, and we want you to come and be with us," Grace assured them.

"I don't know how to thank you." Mrs. Coppock stood at her doorway with the baby resting on her hip. She'd invited Grace inside, but Grace declined the offer. She had to hurry back home.

"Your family has been more than kind to us," Mrs. Coppock went on. "Jason and Mr. Coppock are grateful, as well. We'll come along to your home directly from church."

"We'll be expecting you around three." With a wave, Grace turned back down the path. At last she and Amy would have a few minutes alone to talk.

The air was steamy hot, and Grace was grateful for the shade from her bonnet. How she wished she had a fancy dress with a matching parasol to ward off the hot sun.

When she arrived back in town, she made sure her path led past the boardinghouse. There on the front porch sat Sadie Rose! Grace could hardly believe her good fortune. Sadie Rose was dressed in a pink ruffled frock with billowy sleeves and no bonnet. In her hand she held an ivory fan, which she waved slowly back and forth.

Grace nearly ran in Sadie Rose's direction. "Hello!" she called out. "Hello, Sadie Rose!"

Sadie Rose's lovely face broke into a smile that warmed Grace's heart. "Hello to you, Grace. Come set a spell. How have you been?"

Grace bounded up the steps to the porch and sat down in the wicker chair beside Sadie Rose. "I'm quite well, thank you. I stopped by to see you one day, but Mrs. Kingsley said you were sleeping."

Sadie Rose laughed lightly. "Ah yes, sleep. Something I do when others are awake."

"Are you still singing at Mr. Dunne's tavern?"

"That I am. Mr. Dunne, it turns out, is as fair an employer as I've had in quite a spell."

"I'm pleased to hear that."

"He appreciates my singing and my piano music."

"I'm sure you're excellent." Grace had so many questions to ask. "Sadie Rose, how did you learn to play the piano? Did you take lessons?"

Sadie Rose adjusted her ruffled skirts and gave a little sigh. "It was my dear ma who taught me. Before she died."

"Oh, I'm sorry," Grace said.

"No need to be sorry. It was such a long time ago."

"Sadie Rose, would it be too much to ask. . . ? I mean, well, I was supposed to have a piano. It was ordered, but the bank failures and the dried-up river slowed everything down."

Sadie Rose closed her fan and leaned forward. "Yes, Grace? What is it you want to ask?"

"Could you teach me a little bit about the piano? Just a little? I wouldn't take up much of your time."

Sadie Rose relaxed into her chair. "Why, of course I could teach you. At least a couple of songs anyway. Meet me at the tavern early next Saturday morning. No one will be there then. Can you make it?"

"But I thought you slept late."

"Grace, for you I'd sacrifice my sleep."

For a moment Grace thought her heart would beat right out of her chest. "Thank you, Sadie Rose. I'll be there next Saturday morning."

Grace ran the rest of the way home and barely made it before the family sat down to supper.

Sunday's feast was a magnificent affair. Because Mama's table wasn't nearly big enough, makeshift tables were set up in the dining room by placing long boards over sawhorses. Jason and Drew took their plates out in the dooryard to eat. Matthew, Adah, and Amy's sister Leah, were fed in the kitchen. But Grace and Amy were allowed to eat with the grown-ups.

The men talked of better times and how wise banking practices could prevent such disasters from ever hitting Cincinnati again. At one point during the meal, Grace was surprised to hear Carter say to Papa, "Thad, I want you to know I've changed my mind about working at the boatworks with you and Luke."

Papa's bushy eyebrows went up, but he waited for Carter to have his say.

"I've been doing a good deal of thinking this summer," Carter went on. "It always seemed to me a man could make a go of things by himself. Well, I've tried that, and I've seen my family go without the things they need."

"We've all seen our families go without," came Papa's gentle reply.

"That's true," Carter said. "The difference is, you have something to go back to. I don't. I know the economy will turn around and the river won't be dry forever. I'd have to be blind not to see that steamboats are the coming thing." He paused a moment, and Grace knew that Carter was struggling to say what his heart felt. "If the offer's still good, I'm ready to take you up on it."

It was Luke who answered. "The offer's as good as the day it was given."

Carter nodded. "Thank you, Luke. As soon as you can take me on, let me know, and I'll be there."

After dinner, Papa took down his fiddle, and Grace stood up a few steps on the stairway in the hall and sang for everyone. Soon she had them all clapping their hands and laughing and joining in on the choruses. Hearts that had been heavy with worry and fear were made lighter for having a few hours of fun

Because Grace and Amy were put in charge of all the little ones while the women cleared the tables and washed dishes, there still was no time for quiet talk. But Grace realized she wasn't quite ready to tell Amy about Sadie Rose. Instead they talked about the opening of school, which was set for the next week.

Amy said she didn't care that she didn't have pretty dresses for the new school term. "I'm just anxious to get back to studying," she said. "Mama and Papa and Jason and I have all agreed that things aren't nearly as important as having one another."

Grace thought about that a moment and realized she agreed. Even though she still longed to have her own piano, she knew a piano could never replace the love of her family.

Owen and Samantha left before dawn the next morning. As the empty wagon rattled noisily down the street, Grace waved and hollered her good-byes, remembering especially to say thank you over and over again. She wondered what her family would have done without the generosity of the Tates.

With the new stock of foodstuffs in the larder, Papa was sure they could make it through until things turned around, which he believed would be very soon.

Mama and Deanna continued to make cheese with the extra milk, and of course there was plenty for everyone to drink. Even Luke and Camille took a share.

All week, Grace stewed about in her mind, trying to think of a way she could meet Sadie Rose at the tavern on Saturday morning. In the end, the problem took care of itself. It was Mama who suggested that Grace take a jar of goat's milk to the dressmaker to see if she could trade for ribbon and lace.

Mama had been rummaging in the chest of clothing in the attic. Out of it she'd pulled two of her own cast-off dresses. "I believe," she said to Grace, "there's enough cloth here to make you a proper school dress. All we need is new ribbon and lace." She gave Grace small snippets of the fabric to match the colors.

Grace could hardly believe her good fortune. If it were not for balancing the full jar of milk, she would have skipped all the way to the dressmaker's shop.

Mrs. Cragle was pleased to be paid with fresh milk. Soon Grace had the silky ribbon and delicate lace tucked away in her pocket, and, bidding Mrs. Cragle good day, she made her way down the hill to Dunne's Tavern. As she did, she kept glancing around, hoping no one watching knew her or Papa.

Before she approached the tavern, she heard the enchanting sound of lilting piano music and the clear, full tones of Sadie Rose's singing. She stopped outside to listen, not wanting to break the spell. It was a hauntingly sad ballad about love being lost. Grace stood entranced, wanting the song to go on forever. When the last note died away, she tapped on the door.

"Is that you, Grace?"

"Yes, ma'am. It's me."

"The door's open. Come in."

Pushing open the door, Grace wrinkled her nose at the heavy odor of beer that hung in the air. She'd often caught the aromas outside a tavern, but inside they were a hundred times worse. She hoped it wouldn't make her sick. Across the darkened room, she could see Sadie Rose sitting at the piano.

A little shiver ran up Grace's spine as she entered the forbidden tavern. She knew if Mama and Papa ever found out, they would never understand.

CHAPTER 15

Piano Lessons

"Come on over here and have a seat," Sadie Rose invited. "It's so good to see you again."

Sadie Rose pulled a chair next to the piano stool. Sitting so close to Sadie Rose, Grace could catch whiffs of the fragrance of roses. Roses smelled much better than beer.

Pointing to a key in the center of the keyboard, Sadie Rose told her it was called *middle C*. Then she explained the octaves and taught her the eight notes in each octave.

"What about the black keys?" Grace wanted to know.

"We call them *sharps* and *flats*," she said. "I'll tell you more about them in your next lesson."

Next lesson! What beautiful words to Grace's ears.

"Do you recognize this melody?" Sadie Rose asked. She placed her right hand on the keys and picked out a simple tune.

"Why, that's 'A Mighty Fortress Is Our God.' My favorite hymn."

"Is it now? It's my favorite, too. It's one of the first songs my ma ever taught me. Look how easy it is. It begins on this C up here and ends on middle C down here." Patiently, Sadie Rose pointed out the notes and then let Grace follow her. Within minutes, Grace had the first few bars down pat.

"I don't play this song very often anymore."

"Why not?" Grace asked. "It's so beautiful."

"It brings back too many painful memories," Sadie Rose said wistfully.

"About your ma?"

Sadie Rose nodded. "When Ma and Pa died, my baby brother and I were given to an orphanage in Philadelphia. It wasn't a very nice place, Grace. I did my best to look out for little Patrick, but I had a difficult time of it."

"Drew's an orphan," Grace offered. "He came here from Boston to live with his older brother. I'm sure glad he didn't have to live in an orphanage."

"Yes, be very thankful," Sadie Rose replied, giving Grace's shoulder a gentle pat. "Before Ma and Pa died, I gave them my word that I would always look after Patrick." Sadie Rose paused and pulled a hankie from out of the sleeve of her blue organdy dress.

"What happened, Sadie Rose? What happened to Patrick?"

"People came," she said in the barest whisper. "Came and adopted him. They—they didn't want me. I said I could take care of him myself, but they laughed at me."

Grace squeezed her eyes tight to blink back hot tears. "That's so terrible," she said. "But you couldn't help what happened!"

"But I promised. I promised Ma and Pa. Now I can't even get their forgiveness."

"No," Grace agreed, "but you can surely get God's forgiveness if you just ask. And that's even better."

As though she hadn't heard, Sadie Rose went on. "The couple who took Patrick away said they were coming out West. I've traveled from town to town, looking for him. That's why I sing in taverns."

Sadie Rose dabbed gently at the corners of her eyes. "It earns me enough money to keep on going."

"Why not pray and ask God to help? God knows where your brother is."

"Oh, Grace, you're such a good, sweet girl. But I've forgotten how to pray. It's been so long."

The way Sadie Rose talked to Grace made her feel much older than her ten, almost eleven, years. "Well, I haven't forgotten. Papa reads the Bible every evening, and we pray before going to bed. I can pray for you."

Sadie Rose's face lit up with a bright smile. "Oh, would you truly? I'd like that very much."

"Bow your head," Grace directed. Then she very simply asked God to show Sadie Rose where and how to find her brother, Patrick. Then she added, "And please, Lord, let it happen quickly so Sadie Rose can stop wandering from place to place. In Jesus' name, amen."

Sadie Rose put her arm around Grace's shoulder and gave her a squeeze. "Oh, Grace, you're a good friend. I'm so glad you came to the landing the day I arrived. And I'm pleased to be able to help you learn to play the piano."

They continued working on the melody together until Grace knew it perfectly.

"Next time, I'll show you how to add chords with the left hand," said Sadie Rose.

"I'd better go now. Mama's expecting me." Grace made her way to the back door and gave Sadie Rose a little wave. "Bye now. And thank you very much!"

"Thank *you*, Grace."

With that, Grace slipped out and hurried up the hill. She hugged herself with happiness. She'd actually played a hymn on the piano. And almost as wonderful was the fact that the lovely Sadie Rose had confided in her. She promised herself that she would remember to pray for Sadie Rose every night.

If I were an orphan searching for my younger brother, she thought, *perhaps I would sing in a tavern, as well. Sadie Rose is only doing what she has to do.*

Grace was scolded for arriving home late, but she didn't mind. Being with Sadie Rose was worth all the scoldings in the world.

September's days were no cooler than August's days had been. Sitting in the steamy, crowded classroom at school was sheer torture. Mr. Inman's collar and tie were rumpled my midmorning each day. Periodically he ran his finger around inside the stiff collar as though he wished he could fling it off.

So many things had changed since last spring. Amy was quieter, and she had no new dress to wear. Although Grace's dress wasn't actually new, it was still prettier than almost any other dress in the classroom. How thankful she was that she had a resourceful mama.

Drew now attended school upstairs. Grace missed having him nearby, but she knew he'd be fine. He wasn't a dapper Boston dandy anymore. In fact, at first glance, he looked no different than any other boy at school. His face had lost its pasty color and fairly glowed from a summer of traipsing through the woods.

And, of course, Jason Coppock was in the classroom upstairs, too. He'd keep an eye out for Drew.

Raggy had also graduated to the upstairs classroom, but he seldom attended. Grace thought Raggy looked thinner. If the depression had been hard on her family, she could only imagine what it was like for youngsters like Raggy. And Grace had heard that Wesley and Karl had both left town.

As often as possible, Grace stopped by the boardinghouse in hopes of seeing Sadie Rose. In the afternoons, she might be sitting on the porch catching a late afternoon breeze. Grace would stop and talk with her. Little by little, she was coming to know her friend better. And it was a true friendship. Grace had never had a grown-up for a friend before.

Drew never liked the idea of Grace spending time at the tavern, yet he offered to stay with her each Saturday morning when she went for her lesson. Each time, they took a different route so that, hopefully, no nosy person would see and report them to her papa.

"Mind you," Drew would say, "the more times you go to the tavern, the greater the chance of your being caught."

Grace knew he was concerned for her, but she knew that Drew also liked to be around Sadie Rose. And who could blame him? How could anyone not like such a gracious and lovely lady?

September was drawing to a close when one cool Saturday morning she and Drew were sent to the market. While crops were much smaller than usual, still farmers were bringing in a smattering of fall produce—corn, pumpkins, and squash. Some of the farmers would trade for goat's milk and cheese. Others wouldn't. After selecting three nice squash and several ears of corn, Grace and Drew carried their basket down the hill and stopped at the tavern for a few moments.

By now Grace could play all of "A Mighty Fortress Is Our God" without making a single mistake. Sadie Rose seemed as thrilled as Grace. "I believe you're a natural, Grace. Soon we'll start on another song. Perhaps you'd like to learn a boatman song next."

"I'd like that, Sadie Rose," Grace replied. "Lively boatmen songs make my feet want to dance a jig."

Sadie Rose laughed. "I feel the same way."

"Grace," Drew said to her, "we'd better get home." He was standing by the door with the basket sitting by his feet. "Your mama will have a conniption."

"He's right, you know," Sadie Rose said. "You don't want to worry your ma."

Grace was always reluctant to leave. When she was sitting at the piano with Sadie Rose, she forgot everything else.

Up the street they went with the basket between them. "Step lively," Drew said. "Your mama's expecting us."

Suddenly, from behind them came a loud *whoop*! Grace dropped her hold on the basket and whirled around. There came Raggy, bearing down as fast and hard as he could run. He slammed into Drew, knocking him to the ground and making the basket fly. With one swipe, he grabbed two of the squash and kept on running.

"Come back here with that, you thief!" Grace yelled. "Come on, Drew. I bet we can catch him."

"Let him go." Drew gathered ears of corn and put them back into the basket.

"Let him go?"

"He's hungry, Grace. Let him have the squash." He walked to the side of the street where the third squash had rolled. He brushed it off and placed it in the basket, as well. "Come on. Let's go home."

"What'll we tell Mama?"

"That doesn't seem to be my concern," Drew said almost curtly.

"Are you upset with me?" she asked. She couldn't bear to have Drew angry with her.

"We shouldn't have been in this neighborhood with our purchases."

"But don't forget, Raggy Langler stole from us one time when we were in our own neighborhood."

Drew was quiet for a moment. Then he said, "He never stole anything, Grace. Remember? He grabbed the cloth, but he didn't keep it."

She knew Drew was right about Raggy and about the area of town they were walking in, but she didn't care. She wanted to be with Sadie Rose, and that was that. "If you don't want to come with me to the tavern anymore, then don't. I don't care."

"But your mama trusts me to be with you, so I don't have much choice, do I?"

Now that the basket was lighter, Grace let Drew carry it alone. She walked on ahead, not wanting to talk.

At the Morgans' front gate, they divided the ears of corn, then she made him take the last squash. Drew did as she asked and went on his way.

When Grace stepped into the kitchen, Mama stood in front of her, an accusing look in her eyes.

Grace wondered how Mama could possibly know about their mishap with Raggy so quickly.

But Mama wasn't concerned about the produce from the

market. "Grace Morgan," she said sternly, "I've had a visit from Widow Robbins and two other ladies from the church. They came to tell me you've been spending time at the boardinghouse with a painted lady!" Mama's face looked tired. "Tell me, Grace. Tell me it isn't true."

CHAPTER 16

Helping with the Rent

"It's true that I've been visiting with a lady by the name of Sadie Rose," Grace said. "But she's not a bad person."

Why can't old Widow Robbins mind her own business? Grace wondered as she put the ears of corn on the table.

"How on earth did you meet such a woman?" Mama wanted to know.

Grace didn't want to lie. "The day the keelboats came up from St. Louis after the big rain, I asked Drew to go with me to the landing."

Mama sighed deeply and sat down on one of the kitchen chairs.

"The lady needed help, so we carried her bags. She was beholden to us, Mama. We showed her the way to Mrs. Kingsley's boardinghouse. And you know Mrs. Kingsley's is a respectable place."

But Mama was shaking her head. "The landing can be a dangerous place for a little girl."

"I'm not a little girl, Mama. And Drew was with me."

"Then Drew should have reminded you of the dangers."

Grace thought of all the times Drew had followed her into situations that were not of his choosing. He'd been a good friend, and she didn't want to get him into trouble, as well.

"I take all the blame," Grace said. "I shouldn't have been at the landing. But please believe me, Sadie Rose is not a bad lady."

"You keep telling me that you're not a little girl, and yet I find you've been disobedient and that you've been keeping undesirable company behind my back."

Mama smoothed back wisps of her hair, which Grace noticed was growing much grayer. "When I must learn of my daughter's wrong behavior from others in the church. . ." Mama didn't finish the sentence. She stood up and walked over to the corn and began to pull off the shucks.

"I'll talk this over with your papa this evening. I know he will agree with me that you are forbidden to spend time with this woman—this, this Sadie Rose."

When Mama said the name, it sounded like something awful and made Grace feel hurt and angry. But she kept her anger to herself. Somehow she had to make Mama understand about Sadie Rose.

Grace talked to Sadie Rose one more time to tell her what had happened. Sadie Rose gave a kind smile. "I understand, Grace. Your mama's looking out for you in the best way she knows how. You obey her and be thankful to have such a good mama."

Sadie Rose's words made Grace want to cry. How could things be so mixed up?

In late November, the farmers brought their pigs into town to the packinghouses. The air was filled with the frenzied sounds of hundreds of squealing pigs. At least the packinghouses would be busy, which meant the tanners and the chandlers and soap makers would soon have work. Papa said that little rebounds in business were better than no rebounds at all.

After the first snow, Drew bagged his first deer. Grace went to see the carcass, which was hanging in a tree. It was a big buck, and Drew told her he was going to hang the antlers over his bed in the loft right beside the portraits of his mother and father. Grace never remembered seeing Drew so proud or so happy.

Several of his delicately carved boats now lined the mantle over the Ramsey fireplace. Grace heard Deanna repeatedly praise Drew for his skills in woodworking. Drew didn't seem so sad anymore.

Just as Grace's family had shared their provisions with Carter and Deanna, the Ramseys now shared cuts of venison with the Morgans. Thanksgiving dinner consisted mainly of game that had been killed by Carter and Drew.

Although it was difficult, Grace remained obedient and didn't stop to visit with Sadie Rose. However, she often saw her friend about town. When she did, Grace always stopped to say hello. Or she purposely walked by the boardinghouse in hopes of "accidentally" running into Sadie Rose. In her mind, one little greeting broke no rules. By keeping a close watch and timing her walks by Mrs. Kingsley's, Grace continued to see Sadie Rose regularly.

While the citizens of Cincinnati knew that deep snow meant a full river in the spring, still the hard winter only increased the suffering of those who were in need.

Grace celebrated her eleventh birthday during a January snowstorm. Even though there was no party, Mama and Papa tried to make the day as special as they could. Grace thought being eleven would be so much different, but everyone still called her *Gracie*.

It was mid-February when Grace realized she'd not seen Sadie Rose for about two weeks. The heavy snows of January were melting some, and even though it was still cold, at least a person could walk down the streets without wading knee-deep in snowdrifts.

Every day for a week, Grace made Drew walk home from school by the way of the boardinghouse. Still there was no sign of Sadie Rose. Finally Grace could stand it no more.

"I must ask about her," Grace insisted one afternoon after school. "There's no harm in asking, is there?"

"I don't see that there is," Drew answered.

Her cousin now stood nearly half a head taller than Grace. Deanna often said she was going to load bricks on Drew's head to stop him from growing so fast. But he just kept growing. More and more, Grace appreciated Drew's opinions and his quiet wisdom.

"Would you come with me?" she asked.

To her relief, he agreed. Grace tightened her woolen muffler about her neck to better fight the cold wind as they went the few blocks out of their way to the boardinghouse.

Grace went right up and rapped on the door, and Drew stood by her side.

When Mrs. Kingsley opened the door, she said, "I suppose you're looking for Miss Sadie Rose."

"Why yes, we are," Grace answered. "Is she here?"

The matron of the boardinghouse nodded. "She's here, but she's doing poorly. Been down with the fever and chills."

Grace gave a gasp. "I knew something was wrong. May we see her?"

"I can't stop her from having visitors."

Grace waited for Drew to protest, but he was quiet. Together they followed Mrs. Kingsley inside and through a neat parlor area to the curved staircase. Waving to the stairs, she said, "Second door on the right."

As they started up the steps, Grace heard Mrs. Kingsley mutter something about "getting better soon" and "late with the rent." Grace glanced back at Drew and could see he was as concerned as she.

Grace tapped on the door and heard a weak answer.

"Sadie Rose," she said, "It's me, Grace. And Drew's with me."

The weak voice sounded a bit stronger. "Oh, Grace, Drew. Please come in."

Grace opened the door and saw a small chamber that was mostly taken up with a wide chifforobe stuffed full of Sadie Rose's fancy gowns. Lying in the bed with her undone hair flayed across the pillow, Sadie Rose looked small, weak, and vulnerable. There was no paint now, and her cheeks were nearly as pale as the white sheets.

"Grace," she said, "how I was hoping you'd come. How did you learn I was ill?"

Grace rushed to her friend's bedside and knelt down to take her hand. "I just now learned. I hadn't seen you and became alarmed, so Drew and I stopped to see. I'm so glad we did."

"Young Drew," Sadie Rose said softly, looking up at him. "So faithful to your cousin." To Grace, she said, "I know you're not supposed to be here."

Grace ignored the remark. "Sadie Rose, I heard Mrs. Kingsley say something about the rent."

"I wish you hadn't heard." Tears clouded Sadie Rose's eyes. "Perhaps I chose the wrong time to come to Cincinnati. I didn't know times were as hard as they were." She took a deep breath and coughed. Grace handed her a handkerchief from the nearby table.

"Do you not have enough money for the rent?" Grace asked.

"I kept up, but just barely, until I fell sick. But now I can't work, and I've fallen behind. Mrs. Kingsley tells me she's not running a charity house or a hospital."

"We can bring food," Drew said.

Grace looked up at Drew and felt like hugging him.

"Of course we can bring food," Grace agreed. "And we will." She patted Sadie Rose's fever-hot hand. "You rest now and don't worry about a thing. We'll be back!"

When they came back down the stairs, Mrs. Kingsley was there to meet them. "If her rent's not paid soon," she said, "I'm notifying the officials at the poorhouse."

Grace's hand flew to her mouth to stifle the gasp. Sadie Rose taken to the poorhouse! She felt weak at the knees.

But to her surprise, Drew stepped forward. "No need for that just yet," he said, his voice steady. "Give us a couple of days to see what can be done on Miss Sadie Rose's behalf."

The hefty lady hesitated. "It's not like I want to be cruel," she said, "but I have to eat, too. And I can't afford to keep a room occupied with someone who cannot pay rent."

"Of course," Drew said. "We understand." He guided Grace toward the door. "We'll be back shortly."

"What're we going to do, Drew? Do you have a plan?"

"Part of a plan," he said. "Remember the coins Sadie Rose paid us for carrying her bags the day we met her?"

"Of course," Grace said. "Are you going to pay her rent with her own coins?"

Drew nodded. "It's probably not enough, but it may suffice to calm Mrs. Kingsley and show her we're serious about helping."

"What a wonderful idea."

"You go on home now, Grace. I'll go back to the boardinghouse as soon as I get the food and money. I can take a jar of goat's milk and maybe some cornbread."

"But, Drew, I want to go with you. I want to help Sadie Rose." They'd arrived at Grace's front gate, and she was chilled to the bone. Still, she wanted to go back with Drew to the boardinghouse.

"You can be more help by not worrying your mama." Drew opened the gate. "I promise I'll stop by on my way home and let you know what happened."

There was nothing else she could do, and Grace knew it. If Mama found out, then Grace might spoil her chances of doing anything for Sadie Rose.

Later that evening, Drew stopped by the house under the pretense of delivering a cleaned rabbit for Grace's mama. Before leaving, he slipped Grace a note. When Grace went to her room after evening prayers, she drew out the note. Drew had written these words:

Sadie Rose was thankful for the food. The coins paid a fraction of the rent due. Mrs. K. may take milk for partial trade. We'll talk tomorrow of further plans.

Grace sank down on her bed in discouragement. There had to be a way to help. This was a desperate situation. And desperate situations called for desperate measures!

CHAPTER 17

Grace Takes Action

Grace never undressed for bed that night. She crawled beneath the covers with all her clothes on, waiting for the house to grow quiet. She was determined not to fall asleep. When all was quiet, she got up and pulled on her heavy woolen cloak, first tying her muffler around her neck. Never before had she disobeyed her parents so blatantly. But she simply had to save Sadie Rose from going to the poorhouse.

With barely a sound, she made her way down the stairs and out the back door into the dark, cold night. Gas lamps were lit at every seventh house, and she found herself scurrying from lamp to lamp. It took all her courage to turn down Front Street. While she'd never been frightened there in the daylight, darkness was much different.

Ahead of her loomed the glowing windows of Dunne's Tavern. Pulling the cloak more tightly about her, Grace hurried to the door, where she could hear the shouts and laughter coming from inside. Just as she reached out to open the door, it flew open, and a weaving, staggering man pushed past her, nearly knocking her off her feet.

Taking a breath to muster more courage, she boldly stepped inside the door. Suddenly, the noise subsided and all eyes were on

Grace. Remembering Sadie Rose's dilemma, she flung off her hood and stood as tall as she could. "Mr. Dunne?" she said.

A rotund man with bushy hair and beard came toward her. "I'm Mr. Dunne. What're you doing here, little girl?"

"I've come to take the place of Sadie Rose for the evening."

"What?" Mr. Dunne was at first surprised; then he laughed. All around him the other men joined in the laughter and hooted and jeered at her, as well.

"I can play," she said, lifting her voice over the noise, "and I can sing. If you give me a chance, we can all help Sadie Rose." She looked around at the men. "You'd like that, wouldn't you? To help Sadie Rose?"

"Sadie Rose's had a real spell of it. I suppose she does need help." The proprietor of the tavern clawed at his chin whiskers. "Well, I guess it can't hurt." He waved to the piano. "Have a go of it, little girl. Let's hear what your voice sounds like."

Grace removed her cloak and folded it beneath her on the piano stool. It had been several months since she had learned the hymn. Would she remember?

She placed her hands on the keys and began the first few bars of "A Mighty Fortress Is Our God." When the men heard it, one called out, "Say there, this isn't church! Play one of Sadie Rose's songs!" But another said, "Shush your mouth. I wanna hear the hymn."

Grace ignored them all. Once she knew she had the playing down pat, she let loose in her strong, clear voice to sing every word. When she finished the last verse, there were again hoots and hollers, but now their shouts were in appreciation. "More!" they said, clapping. "Sing it again!"

Grace reached inside her sleeve for her handkerchief. Tying the corners to make a little pouch, she held it up. "Here's where you put the money for Sadie Rose." As the little hankie-pouch was being passed around the room, she sang the hymn again. This time she was surprised to see several of the men weeping. Maybe she was helping more than Sadie Rose by her singing.

The next day when she told Drew what she'd done, he was shocked. "Grace, I sometimes think you can never surprise me with your actions, but I'm always wrong. Don't you know you could have been killed down there?"

"I just remembered what Sadie Rose said about the boatmen. If you try to understand people and not act snooty, they respect you." She felt the heavy bag bumping against her leg, where she'd fastened it securely beneath her skirts. "In fact, one of the men walked me to Second Street to make sure I was safe."

Drew just shook his head.

That day after school, they went to the boardinghouse to pay the money to Mrs. Kingsley.

She cast a wary look in their direction when she saw the coins. Although the older woman asked nothing, Grace was sure she was wondering where two children had come up with that much money. With that payment, Sadie Rose's rent was almost current. They hurried up to her room to tell her.

When Sadie Rose heard of Grace's escapade, she laughed right out loud. "Grace Morgan, you are quite a girl." Over and over, she thanked them for helping. Propped up against several pillows, Sadie Rose had a little more pink in her cheeks. "I know I'll be better now. In fact, after drinking the tasty goat's milk, my insides are settling down for the first time in days."

Grace pulled a chair close to the bed. As she did, something fell to the floor. It was a length of blue flowered cloth. Picking it up, Grace felt her breath catch. "Sadie Rose, what's this piece of cloth?"

Sadie Rose reached out to take the cloth from Grace. "That," she said, "is a shawl. Or rather, part of a shawl."

"Part?" Grace scooted her chair closer.

Sadie Rose stroked the cloth tenderly. "It belonged to my ma. I cut it in half when my little brother was taken from me. I kept one half and gave him the other half. Although he was only three, I put it in his tiny fist and said, 'Patrick, don't ever forget me. I'll see you again one day.'"

Grace suddenly pushed the chair back and stood to her feet. "Well now, we'd really better be going. Mama's expecting me."

"Of course," Sadie Rose replied, "and I'm rather tired from all this excitement." Again she gave her thanks as they left.

"Drew Ramsey," Grace said once they were out of the house, "are you thinking what I'm thinking?"

Drew shook his head. "It can't be."

"But we know that Raggy was an orphan and his adoptive parents died."

"That's true, but Raggy's name isn't Patrick."

"Maybe the people who adopted him changed his name."

Drew thought about that. "Possibly. But what can we. . . ?"

"Don't worry. I have a plan."

Drew laughed. "I'm sure you do, Grace. I'm sure you do."

But when Grace arrived home, any plan she'd had was quickly

squelched. Once again, she was greeted by a very upset and very disappointed mama. Papa was by her side, and Grace could tell from their expressions that it was not good. Papa asked her to come into the parlor, where they could talk.

"Grace Morgan," Mama began, "I truly thought I'd heard everything. Now I've learned you slipped out of this house in the dead of night and went down to Front Street to the tavern. One of the most dangerous places in the city. Grace, how could you have disgraced us this way?"

Papa's face mirrored Mama's disappointment. It was enough to break Grace's heart.

"Mama, Papa, I never wanted to disobey you, but I had to go to the tavern. I had to save Sadie Rose's life. They were threatening to take her to the poorhouse."

"Poorhouse? What are you talking about?" Papa said. "You were told not to go see this woman named Sadie Rose."

"I wouldn't have gone to talk to her, but I hadn't seen her in town for two weeks. When we checked on her, we found she was ill with chills and fever." Grace was wringing her hands and trying not to cry. "Don't you see? I'm only doing what you've always taught me, and that's to reach out and help others. Sadie Rose had no one else. The rent was past due. She even said she was hoping I'd come."

"Whoa," Papa said. "I think it's time to hear this story from beginning to end."

Grace sat down by the crackling fire and started at the beginning. She told how Sadie Rose played and sang in taverns so she could earn money to keep searching for her brother. Grace even had to tell how she went to the tavern to learn to play the piano, which made Mama wince.

When Grace finished her story, Papa looked at Mama. "If the church were more generous with their own piano, this might never have happened."

"Thad," Mama said evenly, "we can't blame others for our daughter's disobedience."

"I know I shouldn't have gone," Grace said. "I was trying to let patience have a perfect work. But I wanted so just to learn a song. And now I can play a hymn all the way through. When I played the hymn for the men at the tavern. . ."

"You played a hymn at the tavern?" Papa interrupted.

Grace nodded, and she saw Papa smile.

"When I played the hymn," she continued, "the men were crying. I think men in a tavern need a hymn, don't you, Papa?"

"They surely do," he agreed.

"Thad," Mama said in a warning tone.

"And Sadie Rose needs hymns, too," Grace said, talking faster. "I believe if some of our church ladies would visit her rather than talking about her all the time, she might just come to church." Grace remembered how pleased Sadie Rose had been when Grace had prayed for her. "I think she truly wants to have God's forgiveness."

"Well," Mama said slowly, as though she were thinking it through, "I suppose I could take a couple of ladies with me from the church and call on Miss Sadie Rose tomorrow."

Grace jumped up from her chair. "Oh, would you, Mama? Then I could introduce you to Sadie Rose."

"I'll see if I can arrange that."

"But you, young lady, will still be punished for your disobedience," Papa reminded her. "Not only did you disobey our direct instructions, but I'm also disappointed that you didn't feel you could trust us enough to tell us about the situation and work with us to solve Sadie Rose's problems. You could have been very badly hurt last night. Front Street is not a safe place for a woman, much less a young girl."

"I'm sorry," Grace said. "I should have told you everything from the beginning."

In the end, Mama and Papa set up a list of jobs for Grace to do every evening after school for a week as punishment.

The next day, Grace could barely sit still in the classroom. The large clock mounted in front of the room moved at a snail's pace. At recess she was distracted and barely listened to a word Amy was saying, even though Amy was reporting good news about her father. She said her father had been able to secure a loan from another city and was making plans to start a new business. In spite of the encouraging news, Grace could think only about Sadie Rose and Raggy. Could Raggy actually be Sadie Rose's long-lost brother?

As soon as school let out, Grace hurried outside to meet up with Drew.

"We'll head down to Sausage Row first," Grace said.

"I hope you're right about this, Grace. How will we find Emaline Stanley's place?"

"Easy. We just ask. In Sausage Row, everybody knows everybody."

"But what if Raggy won't listen to us?"

"I don't expect him to."

"You're not making any sense."

"Just follow me and do what I say."

Winter had been especially cruel to the poverty-stricken areas around the landing. The shacks seemed more dilapidated than ever. As Grace had thought, it was easy to find where the washerwoman lived. But would Raggy be there?

As they approached the small house with its little lean-to in the back, Grace saw Raggy. He was taller and more wiry-looking than ever. She'd almost forgotten how long it had been since she'd seen him. Suddenly, she wondered if her plan would work. But it was too late to back out.

"When he comes after us," she whispered to Drew, "you go one way, and I'll go the other. Lead him to the boardinghouse."

"What a crazy plan," Drew said, grinning at her.

"Hey, Raggy!" she called out. "Still carry your rag with you wherever you go?"

Raggy looked around to see where the voice came from. When he spied them, he spouted, "Why, you. . ."

Drew shouted out, "Rag–gee, Rag–gee! Carries his rags with him wherever he goes!"

The plan worked like a charm. Raggy was on their heels like a pup after a rabbit. Grace ran straight up Broadway, while Drew ducked down a side street. As Grace had expected, Raggy went after Drew.

When she hit the front door of the boardinghouse, Grace didn't stop to knock. There in the front parlor sat Mama and Widow Robbins and two other ladies.

"Come on!" she called out, panting and puffing. "Let's go meet Sadie Rose!"

"Grace. . . ," Mama started.

"Your daughter is a little ruffian," Widow Robbins interrupted haughtily.

From behind her, Grace heard Mama say, "She's just a little more energetic than most girls."

When Sadie Rose answered her knock, Grace was pleased to see her up and dressed and sitting by the fire in her Boston rocker.

"Sadie Rose, I've brought company," Grace said, waving the ladies in and then running to the window to see if Drew had arrived.

"Grace," Mama said, "what are you doing?"

"Mama, I'd like you to meet Sadie Rose." Grace motioned toward her mama but kept looking out the window. Just as she'd introduced all the ladies, Drew came speeding into the alleyway behind the boardinghouse.

"Sadie Rose, quick. Where's the shawl?"

"The what?"

"The shawl. The shawl your mama left to you. Hurry." Grace had no way of knowing how closely Raggy was following Drew.

Sadie Rose stood and walked across the room to her bed. From beneath the pillow she pulled out the cloth. "It's here."

Grace took it from her and flung open the window. Raggy had arrived and was squaring off with Drew, his fists upraised.

"Raggy Langler!" she called out. Raggy looked up at her.

"Langler?" Sadie Rose said. She moved to the window beside Grace. "That's my name—Langler."

"Russell Langler," Grace said this time, using his real name and waving the piece of shawl. "Does this look familiar?"

Raggy stared, unable to move.

Drew, who'd had his fists in the air, backed away, looking more than a little relieved.

Slowly, Raggy reached inside his threadbare shirt, drew out the piece of faded cloth, and held it forth like a flag of surrender.

"Patrick?" Sadie Rose asked softly. "Russell Patrick Langler?"

"Sadie Rose?" came Raggy's small voice. "Is that really you?"

Sadie Rose turned to look at Grace. "Oh, Grace! You were right! We prayed and God heard. He truly heard!" With that, she flew out the door and down the stairs into the snow, not bothering to grab a cloak.

Within moments, the ladies from church witnessed the tearful reunion of the long-separated brother and sister. And there wasn't a dry eye or hankie among them.

CHAPTER 18

"Steamboat's A-Comin'!"

In spite of her very grown-up-looking new dress and matching bonnet, Grace could hardly contain her excitement as she stood on the landing waiting for the *Velocipede* to come into view. The winter snows had melted, the spring rains had fallen, and the majestic Ohio flowed full and wide once again.

Grace looked over at Sadie Rose, and they exchanged smiles. The arrival of the new piano meant that Sadie Rose would begin giving paid piano lessons in the front parlor of the Morgan home. That had been Grace's idea. But Mama had had the wonderful idea to hire Emaline Stanley as their servant.

Raggy would continue to live with Emaline until Sadie Rose could save enough money to care for them both and give Emaline something for her years of care. Then Raggy would finally be able to stay with Sadie Rose.

Papa and Luke had completed one of their steamboats, and the buyer was able to make a partial payment. Papa said that was agreeable because as soon as the boat was launched and in business, the owner would be able to pay the balance. Now the second boat was nearing completion.

Drew and Patrick stood off to the side, talking about steamboats. It had been hard to stop saying *Raggy* and to remember to say *Patrick*. But Grace didn't mind taking the extra effort to learn. Now that Patrick was clean, wore nice clothes, and had enough to eat, he didn't look like the same boy. Since Drew understood about being an orphan, he and Patrick had become fast friends. Patrick was even helping with the piano delivery from the steamboat.

Grace and Drew had learned that Patrick was fascinated with Annabelle and wanted more than anything to learn to milk the goat. Grace marveled as she thought about it. That day at the church when he'd tried to take Annabelle, he'd only wanted to pet her.

Grace realized she'd been just as wrong about Raggy as her mama had been about Sadie Rose. They'd all learned a lesson in love.

Suddenly, someone from far up on the landing shouted, "Steamboat's a-comin'!" The call echoed up and down the public landing and Grace started jumping up and down in spite of herself.

Papa had rented a sturdy wagon, and it was sitting nearby. At last, the proud white boat came into view with its twin black smokestacks pointing skyward.

Presently, the boat was docked, and Captain Wharton strode down the gangplank to greet them. "It's been a long time," he said, laughing and shaking Papa's hand.

"Yes, Captain. A long time," Papa answered. "We've all learned how to be patient." He glanced at Grace and winked.

Then Grace watched as the stevedores guided the crane that lifted the crate containing her piano. Slowly, slowly, it came over to where Papa lined up the wagon. Slowly, slowly, it was let down in the back of the wagon. Grace didn't breathe until it was safely settled. Drew and Patrick climbed into the wagon to hold the crate steady. They seemed almost as excited about the arrival as Grace.

"May I ride home in the wagon with you, Papa?" Grace asked.

"Why, of course, Gracie—excuse me—I mean, why, of course, Miss Grace. May I give you a hand up?" Papa bowed and offered his hand.

As the others boarded the waiting carriage, Grace allowed Papa to assist her into the wagon seat. Papa climbed up beside her, shook the reins, and told the team, "Giddap." Grace straightened her full skirts, adjusted her bonnet, and opened her ruffled parasol to protect her face from the bright spring sunshine.

The wagon clattered over the cobblestones of the landing, taking her new piano home.

OFFICIAL

SISTERS IN TIME

WEBSITE!

Your Adventure Doesn't Stop Here—

LOG ON AND ENJOY. . .

The Characters:
Get to know your favorite characters even better.

Fun Stuff:
Have fun solving puzzles, playing games, and getting stumped with trivia questions.

Learning More:
Improve your vocabulary and knowledge of history.

Plus you'll find links to other history sites, previews of upcoming *Sisters in Time* titles, and more.

Don't miss
www.SistersInTime.com!

If you enjoyed

Grace
and the Bully

be sure to read other

SISTERS IN TIME

books from BARBOUR PUBLISHING

- Perfect for Girls Ages Eight to Twelve

- History and Faith in Intriguing Stories

- Lead Character Overcomes Personal Challenge

- Covers Seventeenth to Twentieth Centuries

- Collectible Series of 24 Titles

6" x 8¼" / Paperback / 144 pages / $4.97

AVAILABLE WHEREVER CHRISTIAN BOOKS ARE SOLD

of the church. We are modeling a justice position we hope others will begin to understand and take seriously as we provide workshops and represent the church at various community gatherings. We put into the hands of commissioners and advisory delegates at the last General Assembly copies of the book *Jesus, the Bible and Homosexuality: Explode the Myths, Heal the Church*, by Jack Rogers, theologian and former moderator of the General Assembly of the Presbyterian Church (U.S.A.). Our mission statement reads, "Proclaiming God's promise of justice and love in Jesus Christ by organizing inclusive and inquiring churches in the Presbytery of Southern New England into a community of mutual support for the empowerment of Gay, Lesbian, Bisexual and Transgender persons, and for outreach, education and Christian evangelism."[19] As the number of churches joining our organization increases, we can presume that the witness we bear through our group ministry is increasing the work for reconciliation, justice, and hospitality.

2. Reexamination of the Bible and traditions. Hospitality calls us to reexamine our own biblical interpretations and church traditions in order to see if they might in some way be part of the problem of limits to a just hospitality. Is our reading and interpretation of particular texts causing us to place restrictions on certain groups, such as homosexuals or women in leadership, particularly church leadership? Is this why we may think that the only way to know God is through Jesus Christ? We must constantly struggle with our tradition to break it open in ways that allow the spirit of Christ's love to become transparent in our lives. Reinterpreting and reexamining Scripture (see chapter 4) can help us as we seek to move away from church traditions and historical biblical mandates that restrict our openness to others, so that we might hear the Word for today. The United Church of Christ is fond of quoting a famous line by Gracie Allen: "Never place a period where God has placed a comma." Also on the UCC home page is a quote from John Robinson, seventeenth-century pastor to the Pilgrims, who said, "There is more truth and light yet to break forth from God's holy word."[20]

In the discussion that follows, there are two strategies at work in looking anew at church tradition and the Bible. The first shows how people within a faith tradition can bring challenges to practices of that faith. The second illustrates how persons outside a particular group can lend support without prescribing the way in which change should take place or what that change should be.

In 2002, I attended a conference on HIV/AIDS held by the Circle of Concerned African Women Theologians in Addis Ababa, Ethiopia. The Circle is a group of about 650 African women who meet every six or seven years to present and discuss papers on a particular topic; as I mentioned earlier, some of us at Yale Divinity School are working in partnership with them. At this 2002 meeting, the Circle women were hard at work seeking to change church tradition and cultural practices so that the sexual taboos and customs become part of the *solution* to the HIV/AIDS pandemic in Africa, instead of being part of the problem. The traditions they were seeking to change were several, yet they did not directly affect all of the participants. One such tradition that came up for discussion was female genital mutilation (FMG), which is performed in some cultures in Africa and elsewhere on young girls as they reach adolescence. According to the World Health Organization:

> In Africa, about three million girls are at risk for FGM annually. Between 100 to 140 million girls and women worldwide are living with the consequences of FGM. In Africa, about 92 million girls age 10 years and above are estimated to have undergone FGM. The practice is most common in the western, eastern, and north-eastern regions of Africa, in some countries in Asia and the Middle East, and among certain immigrant communities in North America and Europe.[21]

A video of this practice, shown at the conference, shocked everyone, especially those who were unaware of FGM. Women from countries where it is practiced, while acknowledging the dangers of the procedure, also worried that if their daughters did not have it, they would not be considered properly prepared for marriage and would then be unable to find a husband. The pain of these revelations and the pain experienced by all of us watching the video were very real. Many wanted immediately to ban the ritual, while others cautioned that condemning another's culture was a serious matter. The four of us from Yale did not offer direct comments in the discussion, but later in informal settings supported those women who planned to move ahead to change the practice. In an earlier day, or before postcolonial consciousness, we might have barged straight into the conversation with our Western opinions on the issue.

3. Partnership and power. In the practice of hospitality, partnership and power go together, and we need to be constantly aware of the possibility/potential of misusing hospitality to demean those with less power and wealth and to make ourselves feel superior. For example, for a number of years I have used my power as an author to invite women from the South who have not published in the West to work together with me in edited volumes or collections. I have also used my influence to encourage editors to publish works by these women so that their voices might be heard in a broader context. Opening doors for publication is for me an instance of partnership and power working together for the common good.

One of the most difficult aspects for me as a teacher in the San Francisco Theological Seminary DMin program for women from Africa, Latin America, and Asia has been trying to work with these women, who are all leaders in their own countries and churches, without using/abusing my power as teacher and white U.S. citizen to manipulate them or demean their important contributions to the course. They in turn have power as educated elite women in their own countries that they must struggle not to misuse, even as they struggle to find access to further education in feminist/liberation theologies. I can't join them as a partner in cross-cultural learning if I do not pay attention to the way my inherent position of power affects our relationships. Working in partnership with their advisers and women in their local situations, seven of them have had their dissertations published, adding new voices to the world dialogue.

4. The goal of justice. Finally, hospitality in a world of difference needs to be practiced in a way that seeks to be just with those involved. God's justice or righteousness includes all the ways God intends to put things right and to mend the creation. In our practice of hospitality, justice includes not only an equal distribution of goods and opportunities, but also the creation of institutional conditions that allow persons to flourish and have a say in the shaping of their lives and communities.[22]

In the United States, the Americans with Disabilities Act (ADA) was signed into law in 1990 and included the statistic that 51.2 million Americans, or 18 percent of the population, are disabled. Many changes were made, affecting us all. Curb cuts made stepping into the street easier for those in wheelchairs, but also for persons with strollers, and older people who have trouble with steps could now safely cross the street. The ADA covers people with all types of disabilities, from AIDS to cancer to epilepsy to depression to learning disabilities like dyslexia or attention deficit disorder. Kathi Wolfe, one of my former students at YDS, has spent her life contending with obstacles because she is legally blind. She calls to keep me updated on events in her life, like the time she went to a McDonald's in New York City to place an order for a Big Mac. She was told by the counter person that she would have to get it to go, as they didn't allow blind people to eat in their store! Of course she talked with the other staff and received an apology, but changing laws is a good way to ensure that people begin altering their attitudes and prejudices.

Kathi is a writer and knows the importance of telling a story well. She notes how important it is for the voice of the writer to come forth, which is

> especially important, if you have a disability, and live in a culture such as ours, which considers those of us with disabilities to be "other"—as exotic as rare birds or esoteric

tropical fish. When you're "the other," you seldom get to call the shots when it comes to telling your story. Either you're left out of the narrative, or someone from the dominant culture tells your story as he or she imagines it to be.[23]

As I have worked on issues of inclusive language, she has often pointed out failures in our language, and particularly the way persons with disabilities are portrayed in literature, "We're metaphors. Sometimes clichéd. Other times stunning, similes for love, death, evil—every quality of the human condition. But we're not us."[24] If the postcolonial discussions in earlier chapters seemed distant from your life, perhaps the issues raised by Kathi will resonate with you. We recognize that people can be just "like us" in some aspects and very "other" at the same time. For instance, we could meet someone who was white, female, and a U.S. citizen, all qualities we would share, and then notice that she was blind, putting her in the category of "other." As long as we consider our own characteristics as the norm, we distance ourselves from those who are different. When we begin to realize that there really is no norm, and that each individual carries a host of varied characteristics, we realize that margins and centers are fluid concepts. Our consciousness calls us to be mindful of those who are excluded, those enumerated for us in Matthew 25:31–46.

Our calling to welcome others in Christ is no easy task (Rom. 15:17). It is an impossible possibility! Just hospitality will not make us safe, but it will lead us to risk joining in the work of mending the creation without requiring those who are different to become like us. One of my final memories of Paul Tillich during my graduate school days in 1957 is of a man who was not afraid of the future, but rather eager to participate in the "more to come." Looking ahead, Tillich sent our entire theology class out of the Semitic Museum into the cool October air so that we could watch *the future space age happening overhead* as the Soviet satellite Sputnik I swept by. He did not see it all, and neither do we, but we know that the future that awaits is one that is surely as chaotic as the past—a future open to the work of those who choose to join in God's intention to restore creation's rainbow of difference!

Questions for Thought

1. Like Amos, God calls us all to speak for healing and justice. What has your response been? Has it changed?
2. What to you is the most meaningful story or example of Christ as God's Welcome for you? Why have you chosen that story?
3. What are the limitations to your own practice of hospitality? How do you see God working through and beyond your limits?
4. Which of the essentials of hospitality are you already working on in your ministry?

Notes

Chapter 1: Why Hospitality?

1. Christine D. Pohl, *Making Room: Recovering Hospitality as a Christian Tradition* (Grand Rapids: Eerdmans, 1999), 31.

2. Max Thurian, *Ecumenical Perspectives on Baptism, Eucharist and Ministry*, Faith and Order Paper 116 (Geneva: World Council of Churches, 1983).

3. bell hooks, *Feminist Theory: From Margin to Center* (Boston: South End, 1984).

4. bell hooks, *Talking Back: Thinking Feminist, Thinking Black* (Boston: South End, 1989), 16.

5. See Letty M. Russell, *Church in the Round: A Feminist Interpretation of the Church* (Louisville, KY: Westminster/John Knox Press, 1993), 24–29, 192–93.

6. Elizabeth Howell Verdesi, *In But Still Out: Women in the Church* (Philadelphia: Westminster Press, 1976).

7. Dr. Russell uses the term "bisexual" as an inclusive description of her sexual orientation throughout her lifetime. She uses the term "lesbian" to describe the status of her partnered relationship from 1975 until the time of her death in July 2007.

8. Dorothy Bass, "Women's Studies and Biblical Studies: An Historical Perspective," *Journal for the Study of the Old Testament* 22 (Feb. 1982): 8.

9. Letty M. Russell, *Daily Bible Readings* (published quarterly by the East Harlem Protestant Parish, 1960–68).

10. Letty M. Russell, *Human Liberation in a Feminist Perspective—A Theology* (Philadelphia: Westminster Press, 1974).

11. Cf. Beverly Wildung Harrison, "Feminist Thea(o)logies in the Millennium," in Margaret A. Farley and Serene Jones, eds., *Liberating Eschatology: Essays in Honor of Letty M. Russell* (Louisville, KY: Westminster John Knox Press, 1999), 156–71.

12. Letty M. Russell, Kwok Pui-lan, Ada María Isasi-Díaz, Katie Geneva Cannon, eds., *Inheriting Our Mothers' Gardens: Feminist Theology in Third World Perspective* (Philadelphia: Westminster Press, 1988).

13. J. C. Hoekendijk, *The Church Inside Out*, ed. L. A. Hoedemaker and Pieter Tijmes (Philadelphia: Westminster Press, 1966).

14. Russell, *Church in the Round*, 124.

15. Ibid., 14.

16. Ibid., 48–54.

17. Letty M. Russell, "Women and Unity; Problem or Possibility?" *Mid-Stream: An Ecumenical Journal* 21/3 (July 1982): 298–304.

18. Pohl, *Making Room*, 31.

19. Russell, *Church in the Round*, 173.

20. Henri Nouwen, *Reaching Out: The Three Movements of the Spiritual Life* (New York: Doubleday, 1975), 79–81.

21. Information on the Circle of Concerned African Women Theologians is available on the Web at *http://www. thecirclecawt. org.*

22. Cf. Musa W. Dube and Musimbi R. A. Kanyoro, eds., *Grant Me Justice! HIV/AIDS and Gender Readings of the Bible* (Maryknoll, NY: Orbis Books, 2004).

Chapter 2: The New Hospitality

1. Gustavo Gutiérrez, *Teología de la liberación, Perspectivas* (Lima: CEP, 1971). The panel was entitled "Liberation Theology and the 21st Century: Celebrating, Past, Present and Future," Denver, CO, Nov. 19, 2001.

2. Edward W. Said, *Orientalism* (New York: Vintage Books, 1979); Patrick Williams and Laura Chrisman, eds., *Colonial Discourse and Post-Colonial Theory: A Reader* (New York: Columbia University Press, 1994), 5–6.

3. Kwok Pui-lan, *Postcolonial Imagination and Feminist Theology* (Louisville, KY: Westminster John Knox Press, 2005), 2.

4. Bill Ashcroft, Gareth Griffiths, Helen Tiffin, eds., *The Post-Colonial Studies Reader* (New York: Routledge, 1995), 2.

5. Musa W. Dube, *Postcolonial Feminist Interpretation of the Bible* (St. Louis: Chalice Press, 2000), 15 (cited hereafter as *Postcolonial*).

6. Musa W. Dube, "Postcoloniality, Feminist Spaces, and Religion," in Donaldson, Kwok, eds., *Postcolonialism, Feminism, and Religious Discourse* (New York: Routledge, 2002), 115. Cf. Iris Marion Young, "Five Faces of Oppression," in *Justice and the Politics of Difference* (Princeton, NJ: Princeton University Press, 1990), 39–65.

7. Musa W. Dube, "Go Therefore and Make Disciples of All Nations," in Fernando F. Segovia and Mary Ann Tolbert, eds., *Teaching the Bible: The Discourses and Politics of Biblical Pedagogy* (Maryknoll, NY: Orbis Books, 1998), 16.

8. Elizabeth Amoah shared this story in an e-mail to Shannon Clarkson, April 29, 2008, upon request for an example illustrating the point Letty Russell had made in lecture notes on postcolonialism.

9. Dube, in Segovia and Tolbert, *Teaching the Bible*, 233.

10. R. S. Sugirtharajah, *Asian Biblical Hermeneutics and Postcolonialism* (Maryknoll, NY: Orbis Books, 1998), 16–17.

11. See "Report of the FTESEA / ATESEA Lectures," Indonesia, March 4–20, 2004, by Letty M. Russell and J. Shannon Clarkson. Minutes of the Trustees of the Foundation for Theological Education in South East Asia, December 9, 2004.

12. Iris Marion Young, *Justice and the Politics of Difference* (Princeton, NJ: Princeton University Press, 1990), 170.

13. Kwok Pui-lan, "Postcolonialism, Feminism and Biblical Interpretation," unpublished lecture delivered at Yale Divinity School, New Haven, CT, Feb. 16, 2004. Cf. Kwok Pui-lan, *Introducing Asian Feminist Theology* (Cleveland: Pilgrim Press, 2000), 16–19.

14. Kwok Pui-lan, *Postcolonial Imagination and Feminist Theology*, 3.

15. Carrie Pemberton, *Circle Thinking: African Women Theologians in Dialogue with the West* (Leiden: Brill, 2003).

16. See *In God's Image* 23/1 (March 2004).

17. Ibid.

18. Judith Plaskow, *Standing Again at Sinai: Judaism from a Feminist Perspective* (San Francisco: Harper & Row, 1990), 107.

19. Robert Allen Warrior, "A Native American Perspective: Canaanites, Cowboys, and Indians," in R. S. Sugirtharajah, ed., *Voices from the Margin: Interpreting the Bible in the Third World* (Maryknoll, NY: Orbis Books, 1991), 287–95. Also quoted in Dube, *Postcolonial*, 18.

20. Warrior, "A Native American Perspective," 294.

21. Rosemary Radford Ruether, "Feminism and Jewish-Christian Dialogue," in John Hick and Paul F. Knitter, eds., *The Myth of Christian Uniqueness: Toward a Pluralistic Theology of Religions* (Maryknoll, NY: Orbis Books, 1998), 138.

22. Renita Weems, "The State of Biblical Interpretation," 31–33 (unpublished manuscript), 1988. Tapes of this lecture from a conference on "Gender, Race, Class: Implications for Interpreting Religions" are available from Princeton Theological Seminary, Princeton, NJ.

23. Letty M. Russell, *Church in the Round: A Feminist Interpretation of the Church* (Louisville, KY: Westminster/John Knox Press, 1993), 162–67.

24. Elsa Tamez, "God's Election, Exclusion and Mercy: A Biblical Study of Romans 9–11," *International Review of Mission* 82 (Jan. 1993): 29–37.

25. Russell, *Church in the Round*, 162ff.

26. Mary Ann Tolbert, "When Resistance Becomes Repression: Mark 13:9–27 and the Poetics of Location," in Fernando F. Segovia and Mary Ann Tolbert, eds., *Reading from This Place: Social Location and Biblical Interpretation in Global Perspective* (Minneapolis: Fortress Press, 1995), 2:332.

27. Sharon H. Ringe, "Places at the Table: Feminist Postcolonial Biblical Interpretation," in R. S. Sugirtharajah, ed., *The Postcolonial Bible* (Sheffield, UK: Sheffield Academic Press, 1998), 143.

28. Advanced Pastoral Studies, San Francisco Theological Seminary, 2 Kensington, San Anselmo, CA 94960, USA; Institute of Women in Religion, Trinity Theological College, P.O. Box 48, Legon, Ghana (IWRC ghana@yahoo.com).

29. Robert McAfee Brown, "Reflections of a North American," in Marc H. Ellis and Otto Maduro, eds., *The Future of Liberation Theology: Essays in Honor of Gustavo Gutiérrez* (Maryknoll, NY: Orbis Books, 1988), 493. Cf. Gustavo Gutiérrez, *The Power of the Poor in History* (Maryknoll, NY: Orbis Books, 1983), 128.

30. Iris Marion Young, *Intersecting Voices: The Dilemma of Gender, Political Philosophy and Policy* (Princeton, NJ: Princeton University Press, 1997), 50.

31. Young, *Justice and the Politics of Difference*, 5.

32. For information on this project, write to: Professor Margaret Farley, Yale Divinity School, 409 Prospect St., New Haven, CT, USA (margaret.farley@yale.edu).

33. Dube, *Postcolonial*, chap. 9, "Decolonizing White Western Readings of Matthew 15:21–28," 157–95.

34. See, for instance: Elaine M. Wainwright, *Shall We Look for Another? A Feminist Rereading of the Matthean Jesus* (Maryknoll, NY: Orbis Books, 1998), 89–92; Sharon H. Ringe, "A Gentile Woman's Story," in Letty M. Russell, ed., *Feminist Interpretation of the Bible* (Philadelphia: Westminster Press, 1985), 65–72.

35. Imogen Mark, "Women of Americas Gather in Santiago," *National Catholic Reporter*, March 14, 1997, 12. Women's Alliance for Theology, Ethics and Ritual, 8121 Georgia Ave., #310, Silver Spring, MD 20910, USA (water@hers.com); Con-Spirando, Casilla 371-11 Correro

Nunoa, Santiago, Chile (conspira@mail.bellsouth.ch); Ivone Gebara, Rue
Jorge Dos Santos, 278 Tabatinga, Camaragibe PE, Brazil.

Chapter 3: Riotous Difference as God's Gift to the Church

1. Billy Taylor and Dick Dallas, "I Wish I Knew How," in *Singing the
Living Tradition* (Boston: Beacon Press, Unitarian Universalist Association, 1993), 151.

2. Walter Wink, *Engaging the Powers: Discernment and Resistance in a
World of Domination* (Minneapolis: Fortress Press, 1992), 77.

3. José Miguez Bonino, "Genesis 11:1–9: A Latin American Perspec-
tive," in Priscilla Pope-Levison and John R. Levison, eds., *Return to
Babel: Global Perspectives on the Bible* (Louisville, KY: Westminster John
Knox Press, 1999), 15.

4. Duane F. Watson, "Babylon," in David Noel Freedman et al., eds.,
The Anchor Bible Dictionary (New York: Doubleday, 1992), 1:563.

5. Mary John Mananzan, Mercy Oduyoye, Letty Russell, Elsa Tamez,
"'The Spirit Is Troubling the Water,' Statement on the Ecumenical
Decade: Churches in Solidarity with Women, 1989" (1990), in Michael
Kinnamon and Brian E. Cope, eds., *The Ecumenical Movement* (Geneva:
WCC Publications, 1997), 224.

6. Sonia Omulepu, "Drafting by Consensus: How the Decade Festival's Living Letter Came to Be," *Ecumenical Courier*, U.S. Office, WCC,
Spring 1999, 11–12.

7. "Together on the Way, 5.8 A Statement on Human Rights,"
http://www.wcc-coe.org/wcc/assembly/hr-e.html, 3.3.

8. Ibid.

9. "Festival: Some Common Ground on Sexuality," *e-Jubilee*, no. 1,
December 4, 1998, http://www.wcc-coe.org/wcc/assembly/ejubilee/
1-piece6.htm.

10. Konrad Raiser, in a press release, World Council of Churches
Office of Communication, http://www.wcc-coe.org/wcc/assembly/
pre-08.html.

11. Louie Crew, "Breaking the Silence in Harare," *The Witness* 82/3
(March 1999): 24.

12. Peter Gomes, "Beyond the Human Point of View," available at
http://www.covenantnetwork.org/gomes.html, or from the Covenant
Network Administrative Office, c/o Calvary Presbyterian Church, 2515
Fillmore St., San Francisco, CA 94115.

13. Justo L. González, "Reading from My Bicultural Place: Acts 6:1–7," in Fernando F. Segovia and Mary Ann Tolbert, eds., *Reading from This Place: Social Location and Biblical Interpretation in the United States* (Minneapolis: Fortress Press, 1995), 1:146.

14. Audre Lorde, *Sister Outsider: Essays and Speeches* (Trumansburg, NY: Crossing Press, 1984), 115.

15. Michael Kinnamon, *Truth and Community: Diversity and Its Limits in the Ecumenical Movement* (Grand Rapids: Eerdmans, 1988), 1–18.

16. Mary Ann Lundy, "Unity and Diversity," in Letty M. Russell and J. Shannon Clarkson, eds., *Dictionary of Feminist Theologies* (Louisville, KY: Westminster John Knox Press, 1996), 305–6.

17. Thomas F. Best, ed., *Beyond Unity-in-Tension*, Faith and Order Paper No. 138 (Geneva: WCC Publications, 1988), 1, 22.

18. Faith and Order Paper 111 (Geneva: WCC Publications, 1982). See Janet Crawford, "Women and Ecclesiology: Two Ecumenical Streams?" *Ecumenical Review* 53/1 (Jan. 2001): 14–24, and Kinnamon and Cope, *The Ecumenical Movement*, 193, 202–3.

19. Best, *Beyond Unity-in-Tension*, 27.

20. "Kin-dom," taken from Georgene Wilson, O.S.F., is meant to represent the coming together of all people—with an emphasis placed on the family ties and relationships that are central to Hispanic culture. ("Kindom" is used to replace kingdom, a sexist and elitist term.) Feminist Sexual Ethics Project, Brandeis University, Literature Review by Laura Hymson. www.brandeis.edu/projects/fse/christianity/chris-lit/chris-lit-isasidiaz.html.

21. See Russell, *Church in the Round*, 172–75.

22. John Koenig, *New Testament Hospitality: Partnership with Strangers as Promise and Mission* (Philadelphia: Fortress Press, 1985), 10; Russell, *Church in the Round*, 173.

23. Best, *Beyond Unity-in-Tension*, 23.

24. Desmond Tutu, WCC Commission on Faith and Order, Santiago de Compostela, 1993, in Kinnamon and Cope, *The Ecumenical Movement*, 242.

25. WCC news release, "Desmond Tutu: 'We Can Only be Human Together,'" 2002/2006, www.wcc-assembly.info.

26. Russell, *Church in the Round*, 14.

27. Omulepu, "Drafting by Consensus," 12.

28. "Letter to the Eighth Assembly of the World Council of Churches from the Women and Men of the Decade Festival of the Churches in Solidarity with Women," http://www.oikone.org/index.php?id=2983.

29. Bonino, "Genesis 11:1–9: A Latin American Perspective," 15–16; Letty M. Russell, "The Church and God's Pentecostal Gift," in Cynthia

M. Campbell, ed., *Renewing the Vision: Reformed Faith for the 21st Century* (Louisville, KY: Geneva Press, 2000), 51–65.

30. Iris Marion Young, *Justice and the Politics of Difference* (Princeton, NJ: Princeton University Press, 1990), 156–91.

31. Ibid., 171.

32. Margaret Farley, "Partnership in Hope: Gender, Faith, and Responses to HIV/AIDS in Africa," *Journal of Feminist Studies in Religion* 20/1 (Spring 2004): 148.

33. http://www.harvard-magazine.com/issues/so96/faith.4.html. Cf. Diana L. Eck, *A New Religious America* (San Francisco: HarperSanFrancisco, 2001).

Chapter 4: Reframing a Theology of Hospitality

1. George Lakoff, *Don't Think of the Elephant!* (White River Junction, VT: Chelsea Green Publishing, 2004), 15.

2. Letty M. Russell, Aruna Gnanadason, and J. Shannon Clarkson, eds., *Women's Voices and Visions* (Geneva: World Council of Churches, 2005), 5.

3. "True Hospitality," *Transforma Mundo*, WCC Ninth Assembly, Feb. 17, 2004, #4:1.

4. Letty M. Russell, *Church in the Round: A Feminist Interpretation of the Church* (Louisville, KY: Westminster/John Knox Press, 1993).

5. Ibid., 173.

6. Rabbi J. Rolando Matalon, "Faith: Conference Aims for Understanding," *New Haven Register*, July 30, 2008, A4.

7. Rebecca Todd Peters, "Decolonizing Our Minds: Postcolonial Perspectives on the Church," in Russell, Gnanadason, and Clarkson, *Women's Voices and Visions*, 93–110.

8. Ibid., 99.

9. Ibid., 97.

10. www.yesmagazine.org/article.asp?ID=1337.

11. John Koenig, *New Testament Hospitality: Partnership with Strangers as Promise and Mission* (Philadelphia: Fortress Press, 1985), 57.

12. Ibid., 8.

13. Ibid., 9.

14. Ibid., 10; Russell's emphasis.

15. Katharine Doob Sakenfeld, *Ruth*, Interpretation (Louisville, KY: John Knox Press, 1999), 10, 56.

16. John H. Elliott, "The Bible from the Perspective of the Refugee," in Gary MacEoin, ed., *Sanctuary* (New York: Harper & Row, 1985), 50.

17. Elie Wiesel, "The Refugee,"in MacEoin, *Sanctuary*, 50.

18. Walter Brueggemann, "Biblical Authority: A Personal Reflection," Nov. 25, 2000, www.covenantnetwork.org/brueggemann.html, 3.

19. J. K. Rowling, *Harry Potter and the Prisoner of Azkaban* (New York: Scholastic Press, 1999), 52–53.

20. Mary Ann Tolbert, "Protestant Feminists and the Bible: On the Horns of a Dilemma," in Alice Bach, ed., *The Pleasure of Her Text: Feminist Readings of Biblical and Historical Texts* (Philadelphia: Trinity Press Int., 1990), 12.

21. "Patriarchy" as a general term in feminist analysis is understood in two different senses. First, as a name given to a variety of social systems of domination and subordination in which women's realities are defined by the status (race, class, country, religion, etc.) of the men to whom they belong as daughter, wife, and mother, and as an interpretive framework or paradigm of that social system in which authority as domination is understood as a description of social reality that justifies the domination of subordinate groups by those who are dominant. "Kyriarchy" broadens this same description to make it clear that domination and subordination or oppression are part of the experience of persons, not just because of gender, but also because of race, class, nationality, and so much more. These social structures are interlocked, and often women are part of the dominant or oppressor group as well as of those dominated, as was seen, for example, in the system of chattel slavery in the United States. Cf. Elisabeth Schüssler Fiorenza, "Feminist Hermeneutics," and Rosemary Radford Ruether, "Patriarchy," in Letty M. Russell and J. Shannon Clarkson, eds., *Dictionary of Feminist Theologies* (Louisville, KY: Westminster John Knox Press, 1996).

22. Mary Ann Tolbert, "Defining the Problem: The Bible and Feminist Hermeneutics," *Semeia* 28 (Atlanta: Society of Biblical Literature, 1983), 120.

23. Katharine Doob Sakenfeld, "Ruth 4, An Image of Eschatological Hope," in Margaret A. Farley and Serene Jones, eds., *Liberating Eschatology: Essays in Honor of Letty M. Russell* (Louisville, KY: Westminster John Knox Press, 1999), 11, 56.

24. Sakenfeld, "Ruth 4," 61, and Sakenfeld, *Just Wives? Stories of Power and Survival in the Old Testament and Today* (Louisville, KY: Westminster John Knox Press, 2003), 35–36.

25. Sakenfeld, "Ruth 4," 1–16.

26. Barbara Lundblad, Beecher Lectures, Yale Divinity School, Oct., 2001. Later published in *Making Time: Preaching Biblical Stories in Present Tense* (Nashville: Abingdon, 2007).

27. Michael Fishbane, *The Exegetical Imagination: On Jewish Theology*, by Lundblad quoted in the Beecher Lectures, 2001.
28. Sakenfeld, "Ruth 4," 55–67.
29. Ibid., 63.
30. Ibid.
31. Musa W. Dube, *Postcolonial Feminist Interpretation of the Bible* (St. Louis: Chalice Press: 2000). Cf. Fernando F. Segovia and Mary Ann Tolbert, eds., *Reading from This Place*, vols. 1 and 2 (Minneapolis: Fortress Press, 1995).
32. Dube, *Postcolonial*, 138.
33. Phyllis Trible, *Texts of Terror* (Minneapolis: Fortress Press, 1998). Cf. also Trible, *God and the Rhetoric of Sexuality* (Philadelphia: Fortress Press, 1978), 166–99.
34. Sakenfeld, "Ruth 4," 87; cf. Delores Williams, *Sisters in the Wilderness: The Challenge of Womanist God-Talk* (Maryknoll, NY: Orbis Books, 1993).
35. Kingman Brewster, "Stories in the Stones," *Yale Alumni Magazine*, May/June 2006, 51.

Chapter 5: Just Hospitality

1. Jonathan Sacks, The Chief Rabbi's New Year Message BBC Online Religion & Ethics (2001), http://www.chiefrabbi.org/articles/other/rhbbc.html
2. William Stacy Johnson, "Unequally Yoked," *Presbyterian Outlook* (May 28, 2001), 11–12.
3. From "Affirmation 2001," quoted by Johnson, *Presbyterian Outlook*, 11.
4. Ibid.
5. Ibid.
6. Robert McAfee Brown, "The 'Preferential Option for the Poor' and the Renewal of Faith," in William K. Tabb, ed., *Churches in Struggle: Liberation Theologies and Social Change in North America* (New York: Monthly Review Press, 1986), 10. For an example of God's just actions, see Psalm 82.
7. Iris Marion Young, *Justice and the Politics of Difference* (Princeton, NJ: Princeton University Press, 1990), 39.
8. Margaret Farley, *Just Love: A Framework for Christian Sexual Ethics* (New York: Continuum Int., 2006), 208.
9. Musa W. Dube, "Grant Me Justice: Towards Gender Sensitive Multi-sectoral HIV/AIDS Readings of the Bible," in Musa W. Dube and

Musimbi Kanyoro, eds., *Grant Me Justice! HIV/AIDS and Gender Readings of the Bible* (Maryknoll, NY: Orbis Books, 2004), 7.

10. "A Call to Covenant Community," www.covenantnetwork.org/ c2cc06.htm. In 1996 the General Assembly of the Presbyterian Church (U.S.A.) passed an amendment called Amendment B, which required "fidelity in marriage and chastity in singleness." This amendment passed into law for the denomination by the necessary margins. The next year the Assembly voted another amendment, Amendment A, which advocated for "integrity in all relationships of life." To encourage people in the presbyteries to pass this new amendment, which would supersede Amendment B, a group created Covenant Network and then circulated their "Call to Covenant Community" for members of the church to sign.

11. Christine D. Pohl, *Making Room: Recovering Hospitality as a Christian Tradition* (Grand Rapids: Eerdmans, 1999), 31.

12. Letty M. Russell, *Church in the Round: A Feminist Interpretation of the Church* (Louisville, KY: Westminster/John Knox Press, 1993), 149–50.

13. David H. Kelsey, *The Uses of Scripture in Recent Theology* (Philadelphia: Fortress Press, 1975), 167–75, 194.

14. H. Richard Niebuhr, *Christ and Culture*, (New York: Harper and Row, 1951): 158.

15. Pohl, *Making Room*, 145.

16. Russell, *Church in the Round*, 178.

17. See Mary Grey, *Introducing Feminist Images of God* (Cleveland: Pilgrim Press, 2001), 72–85.

18. Taken from "Help Us Accept Each Other" by Fred Kaan © Hope Publishing Co., Carol Stream, IL 60188. All rights reserved. Used by permission.

19. "Presbyterian Promise News," published by Presbyterian Promise, Inc., New Haven, CT, no. 17, Sept. 2005.

20. Gracie Allen and John Robinson, "God Is Still Speaking" homepage, www.ucc.org/god-is-still-speaking.

21. "Female Genital Mutilation," World Health Organization, www.who.int/mediacentre/factsheets/fs241/en.

22. Young, *Justice and the Politics of Difference*, 39.

23. Kathi Wolfe, "Whose Story Is It, Anyway?" (Part 2), *Scene4 Magazine*, http://www.scene4.com/html/kathiwolfe0808.html.

24. Ibid.

Index of Scripture References

Index of Subjects